EXCESSIVE FORCE

Force of Nature Series Book 7

By

KATHI S. BARTON

World Castle Publishing, LLC

WCP

World Castle Publishing, LLC

Pensacola, Florida

Copyright © Kathi S. Barton 2014

ISBN: 9781629890579

First Edition World Castle Publishing, LLC January 5, 2014

http://www.worldcastlepublishing.com

Licensing Notes

Cover: Karen Fuller

Editor: Eric R. Johnston

CHAPTER 1

Jodie moved to the decking around the house and took a deep breath. It was hard to be relaxed as she knew she had to be when all she could smell was wolf. She put out her fist to rap her fingers against the wooden door when it opened suddenly and three teenage children came tumbling out. She stepped back just as one of them tried to take her out. The boy looked up at her and winked as he scampered off the deck and into the yard with the others. Before she could turn back to the door, the sound of laughter was cut off and a scream rent the air.

Taking off before she could think, she scooped the kid up and held her hand over the large wound in his forehead. She said a few quick words and laid him gently to the ground. His eyes were closed, but she knew that he was going to be fine. Moving her hand from the bloodied area, she watched as the wound closed itself. A hand on her shoulder had her grabbing it and throwing him off her before she could think. The man didn't move as she stood up.

"He should know better than to grab someone, but sometimes he just doesn't think." She turned slowly, knowing that the man behind her was the alpha and she had just pissed

1

him off. "Did he hurt you?"

"The kid? Hardly. He hit his head." She moved to go to her bike, thinking this was a waste of time now, when the man on the ground stood up. Christ, he was flipping huge. She took a step back and bumped into the man behind her. She hurriedly took a side step to have both of them where she could see them.

"We're not going to hurt you." She nodded at the alpha. "But you don't believe me." Jodie didn't answer him as he continued with a nod. "My name is Austin Force. This is my home. The idiot over there is my brother, Connor. The boy there is his son, Dalton."

"I didn't hurt him either." This time he nodded at her with a smile. "I have to report to you that I'm in the area. Is that going to be a problem?"

"No. But you don't smell like wolf. What are you?" She didn't answer him but looked at the two women on the deck that had come out of the house. "My mate and my sister-in-law, Lou. Would you like to come in?"

"I'm supposed to report to you, not socialize." She flushed when he laughed at her. "I'm doing as instructed. The vampire is said to be here by his housekeeper. Can I talk to him as well?"

"I'm Phil Campbell." Another man was suddenly there, but she didn't move. "You're not a vampire either. And the alpha asked you a question."

"Shape shifter. I'm only going to be here for about a month before I leave. The rest of them should have already come to find the ones in charge, but I don't really care if they did or didn't. I'm finished." She started for her bike only to have the vampire step in front of her. She took a step back before she could think that she didn't want to show him she was intimidated by him.

"You're not just a shape shifter, are you?" Jodie didn't move, but he leaned forward and smelled her throat. She closed her eyes and tightened her lips when she felt her fangs drop. He took a step back and stared at her.

"You finished?" He nodded once. "Then I'd very much like to leave. I've done what I'm required to do and when I'm ready to move on, I'll let you all know."

"You are required to introduce yourself to us, not just come by to let us know you're here." She had forgotten that when the boy had been hurt. She looked at the alpha and the vamp.

"I'm Jodie Turner. I'm staying with my brother's house for now, a house on Main Street just behind the Wal-Mart. They are on their own to find and report to their masters if they haven't already." This time no one stopped her as she threw her leg over her bike. When she started it, she felt the woman on the porch touch her mind.

"You should know that this isn't finished, Miss Turner. You've intrigued them to the point where they'll want to find out more." Jodie turned the big bike around and headed for the gate, not bothering to answer. *"You can run, but you can't hide."*

"Neither can you." Jodie moved through the streets back to town. She'd not wanted to come here, but rules were rules, and she'd learned the hard way that if you didn't notify the other paranormal in the area, they could and usually did hurt you for it. She just wanted this to be finished so she

could get the hell away from her family and back to her own life. Just a few more days, the doctor had told her.

Her father, Curtis Turner, was dying. Not that she really cared one way or the other, but she was required to come to see him off. When her oldest brother spoke, she had no choice but to listen. And he'd ordered her home four days ago.

"He's dying, no thanks to you." She knew as well as her brother did that she'd had nothing to do with his health. He'd done that all on his own.

"He's a drunken bastard and a fucking prick. If he dies, more power to the place he goes to next." Curt had hit her then and knocked her across the room. When she shifted and came up off the floor after him, the only thing that had stopped her from killing him was the fucking bylaws that said she couldn't…not unless he was trying to kill her. She had shifted from wolf to hawk and moved out of the house through an open window, and hadn't been back since. That was two days ago.

"So you decided to come back, did you? What if I told you that you're no longer welcome here?" She turned to leave. "Get on that bike, and it's well within my rights to kill you."

She thought about it for a full minute before she turned back to him. Curt, her older brother by fourteen months, had a way about him that made her want to murder him one second and kill him the next. And to her there was a difference. Murder would be quick, and killing him wouldn't. She stood on the lower step and waited for him to either move or hit her again. He took a step back.

4

"He's only got a few days left in him, and when he's gone, I'm going to make you pay for this shit." She didn't answer and moved into the nasty house. She was glad now that she'd made arrangements to stay at the hotel on Maple rather than come back here. She would bet the place hadn't been cleaned in five or six years.

Her father was a shell of the man she had grown up to despise. He had always been a lot bigger to her as a child, and now…well, now he was still tall, but he had lost a great deal of weight. She stood next to the bed and looked down at him. It was in her power to heal him, but she wouldn't do it. Not now, not ever.

"You should know that I'm getting everything." She glanced at Mike, her other brother, younger by two years. "Curt thinks he's going to get it because he's been staying here, but I know for a fact that it's all mine. You'll not get a red cent of it."

Jodie didn't tell him that he wasn't going to get it either. She didn't think it was the right time to tell them both that she'd owned the property and the house for the past five years, since she'd paid the taxes and had a lawyer change it all to her name. Her father, of course, knew, as he'd had to sign it over to her. He'd tried to contact her about a month later, and she'd ignored the summons to come home. She had been keeping them off the streets since.

Her father opened his eyes and looked at her. She wasn't sure if he could see her or not, but she didn't move closer to make sure. She didn't want to get within touching distance of him. He smiled at her, and she sneered at him.

"You look like your mother." She nodded. "You've

turned out to be very beautiful, mores the pity."

"Dad, it's Mike. How are you? Getting any better?" Her dad didn't look at Mike, but continued to stare at her. "I had her come here, Dad. I told her you were dying, and she came running. She wanted to make sure I wasn't lying to her."

"Have you come to collect? I assure you that I'm still hanging on." She glanced at Curt when he entered the room before answering her father.

"I could care less and you know it. You want to tell me why I'm here?" He coughed twice, and she moved back when blood trickled from his lips. Curt started cursing at her, and she moved out of his way.

When she stepped out of the room, she went to the kitchen to answer the phone. Why they had only one phone in the house was beyond her. She answered with a bark of her last name.

"Turner." Then she remembered this wasn't her house. "This is the Turner residence. What can I help you with?"

"My, you can be nice when the mood strikes you, can't you? I was calling about your family. I just found out who they were and that they haven't made an effort to call to me yet. And they've been here for some time." She started to say to the alpha that it wasn't her concern when Curt and Mike came in the room. Before she could do more than move her wrist to defend herself, she was being tossed against the other wall and fists were pounding at her.

Using the phone handle, she hit one of them but didn't have a chance to see who before her head hit the counter as she was going down. Her last thought was that she was fucking getting out of there as soon as she could.

~~~

Austin was filling out paperwork when CJ came into the clinic. She was spitting mad, and he loved to watch her when she was like this. The two men that were sitting in the chairs were going to learn not to tangle with an alpha person ever again.

"What the fuck did you do to her?" Neither man said a word as she tapped her foot. "I'm waiting for an answer, and if I don't get one, I'm going to start making up my own answers and they'll get you fucking killed."

"You can't do shit to us. You're nothing but a…a fucking female." Austin started forward only to stop when she lifted her hand. He would stay back for now, but one more comment out of the idiot sitting there and they'd need a body bag instead of stitches.

"I'm the mate to that alpha over there, you fucking shit head, and what I say he says, and vice versa. Now, I'm going to ask you again and you're going to tell me, what did you do to that woman?"

"She's our sister, and by laws, she is our property." Austin looked at the two men, then at his mate. He could feel her anger boiling up and over. "You should know that as our property, we can do whatever the fuck we want to her and there ain't shit you can—"

His chair was the only thing that saved him from being a part of the wall behind him. CJ had hit him so hard that when the chair tipped back he fell rather than sailed through the air and became another piece of art. Austin stepped forward when the other man stood up.

"You touch her and I'll tear you apart." The man looked

7

as if he might be stupid enough to try, but he moved back from CJ. "Now, we're going to do this my way. Why haven't you reported to me that you are on my land?"

"Your land?" The man snorted as he helped his brother up. "We don't live on your land. Our father owns that piece of property that we've been staying on, and in a few days I'll own it. So I don't need to report shit to you." Austin watched the two men and felt his brother Dallas step up behind them.

"Problem?" Austin started to say no when Dallas spoke again. "The young woman is making noises to leave here. She said that she'd pay up if someone would give her an amount. I told her that I'd find out how much she owed."

CJ turned toward the little rooms, and Austin told the two men to sit. They tried hard to fight the compulsion, but he was a good deal stronger than either of them ever would be.

"I'm alpha to this territory, and no matter where you live, your ass reports to me. And if you know the antiquated rule about being able to treat your unmated sisters any way you see fit, you would have run across that one as well. What are you doing here, and how long have you been here without my permission?" The smaller of the two men, the one that had been hit by CJ, started to stand up, but he sat when the other one pulled him back down to the seat. "Well? I'm waiting."

"Our father is dying. We came here about…a while ago to be with him and try to make his last days better. Our sister has been out of touch with us, and we finally had to find us someone to hunt her down. She's been here a few days to see him too." Austin felt there was more to his than that but

8

didn't speak as the one continued. "She's a pain in the ass, and she upset our father. We might have…we lost our minds a little and may have hurt her."

"May have? The doctor said she's been beat to shit and that you two didn't stop when she was out cold. You beat her with what he said appears to be a pan as well as a chair leg. What the fuck is wrong with you? Our females should be cherished, not killed."

"She's not a real wolf anyway. Not even a good shifter. Last time she was home, she couldn't even produce a good copy of a bird when Dad had asked her to." Austin turned when his bother touched his arm. "There she is. We'll just take her home now."

"No, you won't either." CJ looked at him as she continued. "She's going home with us. She's supposed to have complete rest and not be banged around like a punching bag."

"She's going with us." Austin didn't bother looking at the other brother again but at the woman as he tried to bully CJ. Jodie didn't look like she should be up and around, much less looking like she was going to take on both of her brothers. Even Austin could see that she'd kill them both before they were able to move.

"I'm going back to my hotel. I don't care for people, and I'd much rather be alone." Austin smiled when she glared at him. "You might be alpha, but I'm not a wolf right now and have no intentions of being one while I'm here, so you have no jurisdiction over me."

He was pretty sure she was right and nodded. He'd ask his mom when he got home. She'd know better than anyone what rules applied or not. He looked at CJ when she shook her head at him.

"All right, but can we give you a lift to your hotel? I'd feel a great deal better if you'd let me make sure that you got there in one piece." She looked at her brothers, then at him. "I won't let them hurt you again."

"Neither will I. But I would appreciate a lift to my father's house. My bike is there, and I want it back." She looked at the older man and glared. "If you touched it, so help me, I'll use your dick as a divining rod to find it."

"We couldn't get it started, and the fucker is too heavy to move without it starting." She nodded and grabbed her head. "Your head hurt, sister dear?"

Jodie moved faster than he could see. When the older man was lifted off the floor and she held the other by the throat, no one moved. She shook them both before she tossed them away.

"You come near me again, you'd better have all your paperwork in order, because when I'm finished with you, you'll never see the light of day again. And I'm not making a threat but a promise to you both." She glanced at Austin and flushed. "I'm going to say goodbye to my father and I'm leaving. I'm sorry for what's happened here today."

Austin nodded but didn't say anything. He followed her out of the clinic and to his truck. CJ was just behind him. She touched his hand, and he knew what she was thinking too. This woman wasn't going anywhere if they could help it.

"She's going to be hurt by them again before this is done." Austin nodded. *"Can we make her stay here? Is there some rule that states she has to stay here before the idiots*

10

behind us try and kill her again?"

"Not really. But I can hold her for a few hours. She's hurt, and as an alpha we can't let her drive off knowing that she's hurt. My ass will be in trouble with the council when they find out." CJ snorted. *"Okay, I'm on the council, but they can still be pissy."*

"I'm calling your mom. She can do wonders with making others see her way. And just so you know, Phil and Holly are at the house too. I think Phil has a few questions for her." She helped Jodie into the truck and got in the front part with him. *"Do you know her father?"*

"I do. He's a nice old man, but I have a feeling now that it's because he wanted me to think so. If there is this much hatred between his kids, I can only imagine how much the father contributed to this mess." Austin started the truck and turned to Jodie. She was out again, and Austin turned back to CJ. "I guess we get to take her home anyway."

CHAPTER 2

Reid Atkins moved on his seat as he answered the last of the questions. He was nearly finished with state boards, and if he got a passing score, he could start his practice. Well, working for the clinic anyway. He put the mark on the last one and flipped it over to the front. He wasn't going to read over his answers again.

The last time he'd tried to do that, he'd gotten every one of them wrong. Second guessing himself was not an option. He knew that he did well, and now all he had to do was wait on the score. Of course, he had to first turn in his test to get a score. He stood up and took the answer sheet as well as the test to the front and turned it in. The proctor handed him his cell phone and his driver's license.

"Good luck," she mouthed at him, and he nodded. As he moved out the door, a slip of paper fell out and onto the floor. He picked it up and stared at the phone number along with the proctor's name written over it. Shelly, it seemed, thought they should get together tonight to celebrate. He started to toss it away and decided that he'd take care of this before she got him into trouble. He headed to the dean's office to let him know.

"You didn't encourage her…never mind. I know you didn't. I've never seen a young man so focused on his studies before. Let me take care of this." Reid nodded. "I want you to know that we're going to miss you around here. I know you'll make a fine doctor and maybe take care of me someday."

"I hope not, but if you need me, you know where I'll be." The dean nodded, and Reid left the office. He was going home.

CJ and Austin had taken him and his brother in when they were nearly starved and down on their luck. His brother Randy had another year to go before he was finished with college. Then he'd be taking his boards to be a lawyer. He'd already set up some internships to work at before taking his final year. They had decided that making CJ and Austin proud to have taken them in was the least they could do for them.

The drive was going to be a long one, but he'd already packed up his things from his temporary home last week and had sent it home with his family. Now all he had to do was get in, gas up, and be gone. He was still smiling when his phone rang.

"You're not going to believe this shit." He laughed at his brother. "I'm home for all of a day, and there are already problems. Some chick is here, and man, does she have a chip on her shoulder about us."

"Does CJ know that you're calling another female a 'chick'? She'll have your hide if she hears you." Reid attached his phone to the headset and started his car. "And what does this woman have a chip on her shoulder about?

14

You by any chance?"

"No, she has these brothers that are going to be on Austin's shit list for a long time if they don't straighten up soon. They beat her to shit because she belongs to them, they said. Not where I come from. She's staying here for a few days until she can get her father taken care of. He's not a nice guy either from what I've heard." Randy paused for a second, and Reid took the opportunity to ask him about other things.

"When do you think our house will be ready? The deal's been closed for nearly six months now…any progress in getting the people out?"

They'd bought a house that had been foreclosed on by the bank, but the problem remained that the previous owners weren't moving out. Nor, it seemed to Reid, did they have any intentions of doing so. At least not from where he stood. He was going to have to call in Phil, and he really hated to bother the man. But enough was enough.

"No, and before you ask, I did contact Phil. I can't do it on my own, but he let me help with filing the paperwork yesterday morning. The courts are going to have to give them twenty-four hours, and then we can have them evicted legally. I hate to do that because of the kids, but they've been living there all this time on our dime." He heard his brother talk to someone and heard the woman cursing. "I gotta go. Miss Turner is going into town, and Austin asked me to take her."

When his brother hung up, Reid thought about what he planned to do first when he got home. He wanted to go on a long hard run. Then he wanted to go for a swim in the lake near their new home. He thought he was looking forward to that more than he was a home-cooked meal made by Nancy, Austin's mom.

The house was too big for the two of them. Way too big, but it was just far enough away from the pack house that he and Randy could come and go as they pleased without everyone knowing about it, as well as close enough that they could run with the pack if they wanted. But the house itself was beautiful.

There were six bedrooms and six baths on the upper floor that also had servant's quarters. There were two more bedrooms with baths on the second floor, as well as the den, and on the main floor, there was a large living room, entertainment room, first level to the library, which extended up to the second level, and dining room, as well as a solarium. The kitchen took up one quarter of the house on that level that the previous owners had outfitted to be able to handle as many as five hundred guests. Yeah, the house was too big for the two of them, but it was all theirs.

Phil had told them that in five years they could sell down and have more than enough money to pay cash for both of them a house, and he and Randy could have a really nice nest egg. Reid hoped it would sell, but Phil told him it would be easy once they made the improvements that were needed. The new roof and landscaping were on the top of the list.

Reid pulled over about three hours from home and got out to take a much needed walk. He'd been so happy to cross into Ohio that he'd only just then realized that he'd not had any dinner. As he filled the car up, he wondered about the woman and her brothers.

He had no idea why he thought of her then, but what Randy had said about her being the property of her brothers had bothered him. He'd read all the bylaws of his kind, a required reading as far as Austin was concerned, and he'd learned a great deal. Mostly he'd learned that when one became an alpha, they had to rule with an open mind as well as a heavy hand. He wasn't sure if Austin followed that rule so much, but he was well respected. And his pack loved him. Reid knew that he did, and Randy did as well.

He was back on the road again when his phone rang. He answered it with a smile, knowing that whatever CJ wanted was hers. He loved her more than anyone he knew.

"Did you know that it's against the law to kill someone because they've pissed you off entirely too much for one day? I just heard that over and over from Austin for the past hour." She laughed when he did. "Please tell me you're nearly here. I've been waiting all day to see you pull into the drive."

"I'm about there. Should be pulling into the drive by the time you're going to bed. I was thinking of simply going to the pack house for the night. Randy said our squatters are still in our house."

CJ snorted. "They seem to think possession is nine tenths of the law. Phil is ready to go in and drain them all in their sleep. The woman who lives there said that she'd move out when the house burned down around her. It was hers."

Randy had told him the same thing. "I guess they're going to have them evicted in a few days. Do you think they'll do anything stupid?" He could see these people burning down the house just for spite. "I really have fallen in love with the house like it is. If they harm it, I'm not going to be a happy camper."

"Neither will anyone else. And they have to know that something is going to have to break soon. The bank has told them over and over to get the hell out. Shit, Reid, it's like they think they're free do as they fucking well please and not face any consequences." He agreed with her. "Anyway, that's not why I called. Did your brother tell you about the woman who's staying with us? Her name is Jodie Turner."

"Yes. I guess she's staying there with you guys because of her family. You must have a full house." Reid hoped she was gone before he got there. He just wanted to rest and relax for a few days. "When will this all be over for her and her family do you think?"

"Soon. Her dad is dying, and he's got his family around him as he kicks the bucket. Lou was talking to Jodie this morning, and she got the impression that the girl wasn't really all that close to him either. And those brothers are peaches. One of them, Curt, is part wolf and thinks he's the shit, and the other brother, Mike, he's just a plain bastard. I'd kill him if he was related to me."

"And the woman? What is she? Randy seemed to think she wasn't human either." He pulled off the highway to take the back roads to the house. He was still a little way away, but he could feel the pull of family.

"She's a shape shifter. I'm not sure what the difference is between a shape shifter and a regular shifter, but Phil seems to think there is one. And you know he's been around forever. But she's nice if a little on the stubborn side." Reid nearly asked if she was more stubborn than her, but didn't.

"She is hurt too, but won't let anyone have a look at her. I think she has a couple of ribs broken too."

"And her father, what does he have to say about all this?" Reid tried not to think about her walking around hurt. For whatever reason, and he was sure she had plenty, she hadn't healed herself. He waited for CJ to answer him.

"He just lies in the bed and looks around. When she comes to his bedside, he perks up a bit, but he won't talk to Austin. He goes with her when she insists on going over to the house. Not often, mind you, but she does go more than I would if he was my dad. Reminds me too much of my own father."

Reid had forgotten that CJ's father was a bastard too. He'd knocked CJ out at her mom's funeral and had told her that he never wanted to see her again. She'd lived with her grandmother when she wasn't driving a truck, and even then didn't even come home when he'd died. Phil had handled all the arrangements with another firm, including taking care of the house that Charles Webber, her dad, had lived in.

They hung up a few minutes later when he was only an hour from home. He told her he'd call when he got there. When he pulled into the driveway, he nearly ran someone down and had to break hard to avoid hitting the beautiful hawk that sat in the middle of the road.

~~~

Jodie sat very still as the man got out of his car. She didn't have time for this shit. She'd come out here to have a nice, long fly when Curt had come out of nowhere and threatened her again. She could have taken off, she supposed, and left him there, but now the man was standing between

19

her and her idiot brother. While she didn't care if he killed Curt or not, she didn't want anyone else to get hurt by him.

"She's coming home with me." The newcomer looked back at her and then at Curt. "She's not going to stay here and sponge off these nice people any longer. Tell her to shift and get her ass home."

"I think she can hear you." She hopped closer to the man and watched Curt. He could be a real prick when he wanted to and would hurt anyone he thought was weaker than him. Actually, she thought he assumed everyone was weaker than him. The man looked down at her again when she turned toward him. But there didn't seem to be anything weak about this man at all.

"She's not listening to me." When Curt took a step toward the man, she flew up and hit him with her outstretched talon. He backed up and the man behind her laughed. She landed near him but not quite in front of him this time.

"I don't think she wants anything to do with you, and I'm pretty sure she's right. Why don't you get off this land before I call the alpha? He doesn't take kindly to uninvited guests." She moved when Curt kicked out at her but not fast enough. She might have been able to dodge his foot altogether but for the fact she was staring at the man. She felt her ribs punch into her lung and knew that she'd never fly away from him now if he attacked again. And she couldn't shift now either. She was entirely too weak and would get hurt by Curt and more than likely the other guy before she could limp away.

The gun was out before she could take her next breath. The man held it like he knew just how to use it, and she was sure he would if Curt gave him the slightest reason. Another man coming out of the woods startled her, but the first man seemed to know him as well.

"Myles, this man has refused to leave the grounds, and he's kicked this woman. Do you know if Austin or Dallas is around?" The good looking man looked down at her then. "Can you fly at all?"

She shook her head, and even that caused her pain. When she walked away from the men, she felt rather than saw the alpha come out behind Myles. He told him what was going on.

"I think we've about had enough of you." Austin took two steps forward, and Jodie had a moment of panic when Curt looked like he was going to shift. "You do it and it will be the last stupid move you've ever made."

"I've asked you nicely for my sister to come ho—" Austin grabbed Curt around the throat and held him up.

"You've asked for nothing but made demands. Now I'm going to make a few of my own. Come here again uninvited and I will kill you. Not injure you little, not hurt you until you bleed all over the ground beneath you, but simply kill you. Do you understand?" When Curt didn't answer, Austin shook him hard. "I asked you a question."

"Yes, you mother fucker, I understand. You're going to fucking pay for this Jodie. I swear to Christ you're going to pay for making me look bad."

The first man laughed. "She had nothing to do with making you look bad, moron, you did that all on your own."

As soon as Curt was dropped, he lunged for her again, and the man kicked him in the face. She watched as Curt crumbled to the ground and lay there. When the man moved to stand in front of her, she tried to back away.

"I won't hurt you." His voice was low, and she felt drawn to him, but took another step back. "Come on. Let me see if I can see how badly he hurt you."

Jodie shifted and took another step back. It had cost her a great deal, and she knew that if he tried to hurt her she wasn't going to be able to defend herself. He stood up, and she realized that she wasn't far off in thinking he wasn't weak. In fact, he looked pretty fit to her. He reached out for her, and she put up her hands.

"You're hurt." Nodding, she looked at Austin as he moved to pick up Curt with Myles. Myles put her brother over his shoulder and took off in the direction that her brother had come from.

"You're able to shift and keep your clothes on. That's amazing, and you're simply beautiful." Jodie looked at him. "My name is Reid Atkins. You must be Jodie Turner. I've heard about you."

"I am. And I assure you, it's all true." She took another step back when he stepped toward her again. "I think you're close enough. I don't want to have to hurt you."

She wasn't sure she could, and he seemed to know it too. She watched him carefully as he moved behind her. Jodie looked at Austin.

"He won't give up. He'll keep coming here until he either gets me or hurts one of your family. I'm going to see to my father. Then I'm going back home." Austin shook his head and turned when he looked over her shoulder. Reid was coming toward her with a medical bag.

"I just want to make sure your ribs aren't puncturing

your lungs. He kicked you fairly hard." She took a step back when he reached for her. "It'll go easier on you if you simply let me do this the easy way."

"Excuse me?" He nodded, and she looked at Austin. "Is he serious? Does he really think I should simply give in to him because he thinks I should make it easier on him?"

"I believe I'm standing right here." Reid took a step toward her and she bumped into Austin when she backed up. "I just want to check your breathing. You seem to be laboring."

"No. I'm okay." He touched her arm, and she tried to pull away from him, but she wasn't able to. Firstly, because she was hurting and dizzy from breathing as shallow as she could, and secondly, because Austin had put his arms around her waist and she felt the pressure building. When Reid put the stethoscope on her chest, she felt something move along her skin and realized it was her wolf responding to him. He must have felt her too because he looked at her.

As he leaned toward her throat, she knew that he was going to taste her. Her entire body was on fire for him to bite her, and she tried to move back from him. But Austin held her tightly, and before she knew it, Reid was pulling her into his arms.

"Let me go." He touched his mouth to her pounding pulse just as Austin let her go. She stumbled slightly, but Reid held her. "Please let me go. I don't want you to touch me. Let me go."

"I don't think so." His teeth scraped along her throat, and when he lifted his head, she could see his wolf. "You know."

23

She shook her head, but he was already lowering his mouth to hers. As his mouth brushed over hers, she heard Austin saying something but not what it was. As soon as Reid kissed her, she knew as surely as she was standing there that getting away now was going to be twice as hard. Then his tongue slid between her lips, and she figured she'd be lucky if she ever got away.

CHAPTER 3

Curt woke to find himself lying on his front lawn. He tried to sit up but found that he hurt in more places than he had names for. When he was upright, he looked at the house and at Mike as he sat there watching him from a seat on the front porch.

"You okay?" he shouted from the steps. "They dropped you there about two hours ago and said you'd been banned from the property. That one guy, the vampire that tossed you there, said to tell you if you come back he'll drain you."

Fucking bastards hadn't paid him the respect that he deserved. He stood up and felt his head spin a little before he was able to move to the porch. He dropped in one of the chairs there and heard it groan under his weight. Fucking fast food was going to kill him, but there was no one to cook for them anymore now that there wasn't any money for a cook. He glared at Mike as he drank a cup of coffee from a local dive.

"You think to get me a cup?" Mike shook his head and grinned. "Then I suggest you either get me a cup or give me yours. Either way, I'm going to have some coffee."

Mike tipped the cup over. "Empty. Too bad. And I've no

25

money to go and buy one either. Like you, I've taken some time off to be with Dad while he moves from this world to the next."

Curt snorted. "Like you fucking care which world he's in. And just so you know, I'm still drawing my check...well, half of it anyway. I'm on medical leave for the time being."

Actually, he wasn't employed at all. He'd lost his job so long ago that he couldn't even remember who it was he'd been working for. He knew that he'd been in management the last he remembered, but not where. It had been probably more than fifteen years since he'd held down any sort of job. Living off his dad's social security had been a bitch, but after the old shit died, he was going to sell this piece of shit property and live like he wanted. Fuck the other two. His brother and sister were on their own.

He didn't think, however, that Jodie needed him or his money. She drove that nice bike, and she had some money on her all the time it seemed. And she was staying at the nice hotel downtown, the one that wouldn't let him in to see her when he'd gone there after she'd just arrived. He looked in the yard for her bike, wondering if he could sell it before she returned.

"They took it with them when they left." He looked at Mike. "Her bike, those men that brought you here, took it with them when they left. Don't know how they started it, but it fired right up and they drove off with it. The vamp said he was taking it, and if I had a problem with it, I could try and stop him. Man that fucker is big."

He was strong, too, as a matter of fact. Curt looked around the yard and wondered when was the last time the fucking thing was cut. Things were gonna have to be cleaned up before he could hope to sell this place. And it probably wouldn't hurt to have a coat of paint slapped on the house either. He tried to think where he could steal some of that as well as a few other things when he realized his brother was talking.

"…sometime tomorrow. I didn't think she'd come back after the beating you gave her, but he said she would." Curt asked him what the fuck he was talking about. "The doctor. He's coming here tomorrow to see Dad. He's going to be here sometime in the morning, and he wants to talk to all of us. I said I didn't think Jodie would be here, and he said she would."

"When did you talk to him? And since when do doctors make house calls to a place like this one?" He knew that his father lived in not the worst part of town, but fairly close. "Who's paying him, too?"

"The alpha called here about ten minutes ago and told me. He said that he's footing the bill and he'd expect us to be on our best behavior or else." Mike handed him the scrap of paper with a phone number on it. "I don't know where the fuck he gets off telling us to behave in our own home, but he said we'd better."

"You know as well as I do that he's the alpha and can pretty much do as he fucking pleases. And if he wants to send a doctor out here, we can't do shit about it. Not yet at any rate. Once Dad is dead, we can tell him to fuck off." Mike nodded and Curt knew that he had no idea what the hell was going on. "What is he like tonight?"

Curt couldn't believe how long his dad was taking to

fucking die. He'd been on his last legs for over three months now, and it was starting to get on his last nerve. *Die already will you*, he thought. He couldn't hurry it along any more than he'd been doing already without causing people to start asking questions. And having Jodie and a new doctor there, he was having a hard time figuring out how to slip him any more poison…at least not as much as he'd been giving him. Maybe he'd give him enough tonight to finish him off during the night and there'd be no need of a visit from the doctor.

"I don't know. Sometime tomorrow is all I know. That guy said that if you had any questions to call him. I don't care when he comes so long as he tells us when Dad's going to die. I'm sick to death of waiting on him hand and foot." Curt looked at his brother, thinking he'd never lifted a hand to give their dad even a tissue. But then neither had he.

"I've got work to do." *Yeah*, he thought to himself, *killing off old Dad*. "Let me know when they get here in the morning. I'm thinking of sleeping late."

"I'll do that." As Curt walked away, he had a feeling that Mike wasn't going to wake him at all and decided to set his alarm for very early. He moved toward the car his dad had had for the past fifteen years.

As he made his way into the tiniest town he'd ever seen, he thought about growing up there. There was a gas station, a library, and one grocery store. And the store had very little going for it…a few things that he'd never eat and a nice selection of weed killer. That's where he headed now.

"You have a slug problem?" He glanced at the woman standing next to him. "We had them for a little bit on our strawberries, but I put out some lime and no problems again."

28

"Yeah, slugs, but I don't like using lime." He picked up the first bottle of killer and tried to ignore the woman standing next to him. She was a wolf, he knew that, but he didn't really give a shit right now. When she moved away, Curt went to the cashier and paid for his purchase. As he moved out of the store, he saw the alpha standing next to his car.

"You should know that I've still not heard from you that you're on my territory. And since you seem to know all the rules of our kind, you should be well aware that I am well within my rights to kill you right now." He moved with extraordinary speed and was within inches of his face. "You might want to make sure you do it as soon as possible before I get all pissy with you."

He wanted to tell him to bring it on but was terrified the man would do just that. He didn't step back, as he had an overwhelming urge to drop to his knees and beg for forgiveness. Instead, he tried not to notice the sweat rolling down his back and across his forehead. He would bet anything that Austin knew just what he was feeling. When he stepped back, Curt wanted to let out his breath, but the smile on Austin's face made him hold onto it just a little longer.

"Austin?" Both men turned to the woman in the store who'd bothered him. "Can you help me? And Billy is bringing out the rest of the things today."

"Curt Turner, I'd like for you to meet my mother, Nancy Force. Mom, this is the prick I was telling you about. He's Jodie's brother, one of them anyway." Nancy nodded at him but said nothing as Austin continued. "He's been trying to

29

get Jodie to come home with him."

"She'll not be coming home with you now, I think. She's got things going on right now that you won't understand." She laughed a little and handed Austin a large bag. "She's a lovely girl. What happened to you and your brothers? Different parents?"

He opened his mouth to tell her to fuck off, but Austin cleared his throat, and he decided that he'd get her later. Picking up one of the bags from her cart, he handed it to Austin with a little more force than necessary. When he walked away, he heard them both laughing, and he felt his wolf stir along his skin. He got in the car and started it. He was nearly home again when he realized that he no longer had his poison, and just knew that it was now in the back of the huge truck that the alpha had been leaning against.

~~~

"I don't think you understand what's going on here." Jodie looked at Reid and waited for him to explain whatever he thought she didn't understand again. "You're my mate, and as such, I need for you to be safe. Understand?"

"You know I'm not nearly as ignorant as you seem to think I am. I understand a great deal, and one of them is this whole mate business. But without my permission, and I've never given it to you, you can't claim me." She stood up, and so did he. "I'm going back to my hotel now. It's been really…nice here, but I've got a great many things to do before my father passes."

"You and I are supposed to go there this morning. You heard Austin. He wants me to see what, if anything, I can do to help him. Or if failing that, make sure his passing is

30

relatively painless." She snorted at him. "You don't want him to have a painless death?"

"I could care less how he goes from this life and on to hell. I'm only here because when he does pass on, I'm going to have to sell off the property and make sure my brothers are put out of the house before the thing is bulldozed." He looked over her shoulder, and she reached out to the woman behind her. CJ again. That woman could come and go like she was walking on air.

"You two fighting again? Christ, why don't you just go up to the bedroom, get this marking and claiming shit over with, and get on with your lives?" She pulled three glasses out of the cabinet and then reached in the fridge for the tea. She poured the first glass and handed it out to her.

"I don't drink tea, hot or cold." CJ raised her brow at her. "Thanks, but no thanks."

"Better, but not great. Sit down, the two of you." Neither of them moved, and when CJ repeated herself, Reid sat, but she moved to the door. "I want a word with you before you go to the house. Austin thinks that your brother is killing your dad. Were you aware of that?"

She'd thought so, but hadn't been able to find anything in the house. There were some gardening supplies in the garage, but it had been so covered with dust that she figured no one had touched it for at least five years. Her father had only been dying for the past five months. She turned to look at CJ but didn't move toward the table.

"You know this how?" CJ pointed to the chair. "I can hear you just fine from here. You have something to say, then say it. I've got to get to the lawyers' office before ten and see if he can do what needs to be done for me."

"About that, did you know that Phil is a great attorney? He is, and he's been looking into what's been going on over there for you. Were you aware that your brothers both think that they're going to inherit the house and all the property?" Jodie nodded. "Ah, so you've not told them that your father signed it all over to you when you paid off the taxes. He might live longer if they knew. Or do you care?"

"Not particularly. He's as much a prick as his sons. At least he had been until he got sick." Jodie turned to the table where they both still sat. "What business is this of yours anyway? It's not like we're friends. And I'm reasonably sure we've never met before the other day. So again I ask, what do you care?"

"About him? I don't care about him. And I'm well aware of what sort of person your father is. He and my own father were best buddies. It's really too bad my father didn't realize that old man Turner was something he despised more than he did me."

"Webber? You're Webber's daughter?" She nodded, and Jodie knew her whole life history in that second. "Your dad was a real peach. He hit me once when I was just a kid. He took exception to me walking on the sidewalk in front of his house."

"Yeah, he was a real shit. Your father isn't much better from what I remember." Jodie looked into the yard where her bike was sitting while CJ continued. "I'd very much like it if you sat down and let us discuss what might be going on over there. Phil is going with you by the way. He's got permission from your own attorney. They're good friends."

As if he was summoned, Phil walked in the house. Jodie looked at Reid when he stood up and gave the large vampire a hug. She took a step back when Phil came toward her. He sniffed the air around her and turned to Reid.

"So, she's your mate." Jodie rolled her eyes and looked out the door again. "You should know that I'm impressed by you."

She wondered who Phil was talking to and turned to see that he was speaking to her. "Me? What did I do to impress you? I'm just trying to get back to my hotel to take a shower."

The images of being naked in the shower made her look at Reid. An image of him naked with her in the shower made her take another step back. When he stood up, she knew that he had somehow realized what she'd been thinking.

"Don't." He stopped moving toward her and she went to the door. "I swear if you touch me again I'll hurt you. You seem like a nice guy and all but I've got a life and it does not involve having you hanging around me for the rest of my life."

"You think that's going to make this go away?" She knew it probably wouldn't but nodded anyway. "You're kidding yourself if that's what you think. We're fated to be together whether you like it or not. I, for one, would like to pursue this to see what we can be together."

"You see this is where we differ. I know what the conclusion will be. You'll find out just what I am and decide that all the money offered to sell me off is much better than having an easy fuck. Well, been there and done that, asshole, and I've had my fill of men like you." She wrapped her hand around the door handle and reached for an animal, any one that would get her away from there. But he wrapped his arms around her just as her hawk took her.

She had no idea what might have happened if he hadn't held her at that moment. But she knew as surely as she was now perched on his arm that had he not, she would have been hurt if not killed. The shot that rang out was still vibrating across the wind even as the wood splintered from the wall where her head would have been.

She knew she was hurting him but couldn't let go of him just yet. Her talons were sharp, but she knew that if she let go, she'd fall to the floor, and she needed to think right now. She looked up at Austin when he stepped into the room. CJ had been moved to the other side of the room by some force. She didn't want to think about what would have happened if she had left the house first instead of her.

"You all right?" CJ nodded to Austin, and he turned to Reid and her. "Good. What the fuck is going on? Was that a shot I heard?"

"Someone shot at Jodie." She moved to the floor and shifted again as Reid continued talking to Austin. "She was just getting ready to leave when I stepped up behind her. I'm not sure where the shot came from, but I would say fairly close."

"I'd like to go now." Both men shook their head, but otherwise ignored her. "Maybe I should rephrase that, I'm going to leave. As I have said several times, I've got things to do."

"Your brother purchased three bottles of chemicals this morning. He paid cash and had on gloves this time." Jodie looked at Phil, and he nodded at her. "I've a contact

34

at the store. What would a man who hasn't picked up as much as a dishcloth in a decade be doing with so much lawn chemicals?"

She didn't like her father, her brothers either, but to know or to think that they'd be capable of killing off one another made her sad and pissed. She went out the door and toward her bike. She didn't get on it just yet but thought about what was going on. She didn't turn when she felt someone, Reid, come up behind her.

"They'll kill him off and get away with it. Then they'll try to kill me if they think they can get the land." She turned to him. "Do you know how much I've had to sacrifice to pay off those taxes? All my savings, and then some. It's taken me almost three years to put it all back in the bank. I've given up so much just for those bastards to treat me like shit."

Before he could say anything, if he would have, she swung her leg over the bike and started it. She was moving down the drive and out the large gates before she let the tears fall.

CHAPTER 4

He was being poisoned, there was no doubt about it. Reid looked up at Phil and nodded once. Phil moved to the foot of the bed and braced his arms over his chest. No one would get past him unless they were set on being killed. Reid looked at Jodie, who had shown up not ten minutes after he had.

She'd changed her clothes. Not to say that she'd been wearing the same thing every time he'd seen her, but she'd dressed up. She'd had on a pair of jeans and a baggy tee-shirt yesterday, and now she had on a pretty silk blouse that fit her like it had been poured over her and molded to her body. The skirt was short, but not too short, and her bare legs looked long and smooth. He had to bite his hand when she'd bent to lay her purse on the chair just inside the room. Reid had to concentrate hard on what he was there for and not what he'd wanted to do to the beautiful woman in front of him.

"I'll have him taken to the hospital where I live. Maybe they can, I don't know, take some of this poison out of him." Reid shook his head as soon as she said she was taking her father away. "Then what do you suggest? I leave him here until they finish what they started? Not fucking likely."

"I'll have him transferred to the clinic where I can keep an eye on him." And her too, he thought to himself. "Then when he's better, we can make arrangements to have him set up in one of the homes close to where we can keep him safe."

"And you'll do this why? For sex? No thanks. I've enough to deal with on my own." She pulled out her cell phone and he stepped to her, no longer caring to be nice. She was his, damn it.

Reid jerked her around and slammed his mouth over hers. She dug her nails into his arms enough that he felt the pain of it, but her body fit against him when he pressed her to the wall behind her. She moaned when he cupped her ass, and he lifted her against his hardening cock. Christ, he wanted her right fucking now.

Jodie curled her fingers into his hair, and he moved his mouth down her jaw to her throat. He tasted her need, as it seemed to pour from her. When she tilted her head for him, he took a small nip at her hot skin and licked the area with his tongue. He wanted to bite her, wanted to mark her, but he couldn't do that, not like this. Phil clearing his throat had him lifting his head from her pounding pulse.

"You have an audience. I'm sure I know what you're feeling, but right now we have more important…well not more important, but certainly more pressing things to deal with." Phil laughed when he growled at him. "I wish I could let you finish what you've started, but the brothers are coming and I don't think they should see you feeling up their sister right now."

Reid looked at Jodie, who was looking at the wall to her

right. He said her name softly twice, and when she ignored him, he lifted her chin to have her look at him. He could see her wolf stirring in her eyes, and his own curled himself around him as well.

"I'm sorry." She frowned. "I was angry that you dismissed me so quickly, and I lost my temper. I should never have…."

"Should never have what?" Her voice was husky and full of promise, and he wanted to pick up where they'd stopped. But he heard her brothers coming up the stairs.

"Your brothers are finally awake. What do you want to do about this?" She looked at him, and he waited, trying his best not to order her to let him take care of this. He had no doubt that she could handle much more than this, but he wanted to do it for her. Knowing that would piss her off more, he kept his mouth shut. For now.

Mike came in the room first, still in a pair of baggy dirty pants and no shirt. Barefooted, he nearly fell as his feet slipped on the rug. Curt came into the room next, wearing nothing but a pair of boxers that looked like they were two or three sizes too small. They, too, were dirty, but it was the look on his face that had Reid stepping in front of Jodie.

"What the fuck is going on here? What are you doing in my house?" Jodie started to step around him, but a growl slipped from his mouth before she could move. Everyone looked at him.

"You might want to take it down a notch there, buck-o. I'd hate to have to hurt you for pissing me off." Phil moved toward the two younger men as he continued. "You were informed that we were coming. And as for your house? I wasn't aware that you owned this property. I just assumed, like most, that your father owns it."

Reid watched the two men and saw the anger being replaced with fake concern. Mike had been doing the poisoning. He'd bet his life on it. And when he looked at Mike, he wondered if he was trying to kill Jodie. These two were bad news.

"I'm having father moved to the clinic. The ambulance is on its way, isn't it, Mr. Campbell?" Phil winked at her and pulled out his phone as Jodie moved around him toward the brothers. "You'll be out of this house by the end of the week. If not, I won't be responsible for what happens to you when the bull—"

"You can't order me out of this house. When Dad is gone, I'll own this place and you're not taking him anywhere. He's staying here." Curt crossed his arms over his chest and glared at her. "You just try it and see what happens."

Before he could move, Curt was slammed against the wall. No one had moved, and when Mike stepped toward them, he joined his brother. Neither man spoke, but Reid knew it was more likely due to her magic rather than them learning to keep their mouth shut.

"I own this place as of five years ago. I've been paying all the bills and keeping the taxes paid up. The utilities as well. And as of now you're no longer going to freeload off me." She slammed them twice more against the wall without so much as moving her finger. "And I will take him where I think he'll be safe from either of you. Unless, of course, you want to tell me which one of you are giving him poison?"

Neither man made any kind of indication they were

going to answer her. Jodie turned to him, and he had to bite his inner lip or laugh. Christ, she was amazing. And powerful. It meant that she didn't need him to protect her, but he was going to enjoy watching her take on her family.

The medics from the clinic arrived fifteen minutes later. As they were loading up her father, he looked at the two men as soon as Jodie let them free. He waited until the ambulance was pulling away before he spoke to them.

"I know." Neither man moved, but he could feel the fear. "You've been poisoning him for a very long time, and now you're going to be fucked because I plan to find out which one of you has been doing it. And I'm also going to find out which one of you shot at her." With that, he moved out of the room and into the living room where Phil and Jodie were waiting.

"You ready to go?" Phil nodded, but Jodie watched her brother's move up the stairs, still dressed as if they were going back to bed instead of starting the day. They paused when Jodie said their names.

"You'll have until Friday. You'll be given a notice today, and whether you're here to get it or not, I frankly don't care."

Phil stood by him as Jodie left the house. Reid turned back to the two men and looked at them. He knew what sort of men they were, men like his father had been. Lazy and mean men who would toss out their own sons so their welfare checks and food stamps would go further without them in the house.

"You come near her again, I will kill you." Mike sneered at him, and Curt flipped him off. "You think I'm kidding you? She's my mate, and I'll do whatever it takes to protect her."

"You think I'm afraid of you, pup? I've beaten the shit out of bigger men than you'll ever hope to be." Curt moved down the steps toward him as he continued. "You'll be smart and stay away from her from now on. If this deal with the house and property is true about what she's saying, I'll have my way or she'll not be much good to you either."

Reid lunged at the man and laughed when he fell back in an effort to get away from him. When he stood up, Reid turned his back on him and left the house. Jodie was just getting into a cab when Phil put his hand on his arm.

"I'd let her go for now. You have to settle a few things before you can bring her back. Like the house." Reid wanted to go after her but knew that Phil was right. He didn't have a home for them and living in the pack house was not an option. "The people that are still living in your house would like a word with you."

"Now?" Phil nodded as they went to his car. "All right. I want a home to come home to, not this mess that I seem to have right now. Is Randy meeting us there?"

"No. Randy has…he's had second thoughts about this house. He spoke to me right before I left, and he wants to live on his own." Phil turned to look at him, as Reid had stopped moving. "It'll be all right."

"I can't afford this house on my own." He felt his heart begin to pound. "The only way we were able to swing this is because we were both going to be footing the bill. Now with him out of it, I can't do this."

"You can and you will. I have a plan." Reid got into the passenger's side of his car, and Phil at the wheel. Phil grinned at him. "You'll need to get something more reliable if you have children. This will never do."

They drove in mostly silence. After the shock of his brother wanting to back out, Reid was working on trying to figure out how to get the bank to take it back without ruining his credit. When they pulled up in front of the house, all Reid could see was how much money it was going to take to make the house right. Money he didn't have now.

The Fields came out of the house just as soon as they pulled to a stop. Mr. Fields had never been overly friendly with him, and Mrs. Fields a little too friendly. Reid was glad that Phil was with him as a buffer between the two of them and him.

"Mr. Atkins, nice day, huh?" Reid nodded, shocked at the man's sudden nice demeanor, and took his hand when he'd put it out there. "I was wondering if you and I could have a talk about the house. You don't really need your lawyer. You and me and the missus can settle this, I think."

"As you can see, we've come together. So whatever you have to say, I'll be here as well." Anger blasted at him from the man as Phil smiled at him. There was something going on here, and he didn't know what, but he had a feeling that Phil did.

"I would like to speak to him alone." Now this was the Mr. Fields that Reid knew. A prick and ill tempered. "Why don't you wait in the car?"

"He stays with me." Phil smiled at them both, and Reid looked at the house. "You've been asked several times to keep the place up. I don't see that you've even mowed the lawns. But then, of course, you were supposed to be out long before now, and I would be mowing my own lawn, isn't that right?"

Mr. Fields looked back at his wife, then at him. That's when Reid noticed that she was wearing next to nothing, and she looked like she might have had a black eye. Reid had a feeling that he was going to be in trouble, more than he could get out of right away, if he even came close to either of them.

"You really should come on in the house." Reid shook his head and backed up. "Mother fuck, how the hell is this supposed to work if he won't do what I tell him?"

"Just fucking hit them both." Mrs. Fields tore at her blouse to where her breast was exposed along with the dark bruise on her ribs. "We can get a deal on getting them both and never have to worry about money again."

"Have you figured it out yet?" Reid nodded at Phil's whispered comment. *"Good boy. Now this is what we're going to do. We're going to get into the car before either of them comes closer. That way we have no DNA on us when this shit goes down."*

They moved backwards toward the car, both of them keeping an eye on the couple who were arguing about how to get Reid into the house. When they slammed the doors shut and started the car, both ran after them, but it was too late.

"They were going to accuse me of hurting her." Phil nodded as he took a turn a little too sharply. "What the hell was that for? I don't have anything?"

"You have more than they do at the moment. Their house, for one. And I put a sizable amount of money in your account some time ago that you've never touched."

44

"That's not my money." Phil glanced at him. "I didn't want that money, and you knew it. My parents never wanted us in the first place, and I certainly don't want their money now."

His parents had won the lottery about four years after he and Randy had started living with the Forces. And when a horrific accident had taken both his parents' lives, most of the money was still in their account. Austin, with Phil's help, had petitioned for them to receive it as they were their only living relatives. He and Randy both had gotten all the money, and both insurance policies had paid double as they were killed in an accident. There was just over seven million dollars in each of their accounts.

"Well, I'm sorry, Reid, but you'll have to use it now. The house will need to be paid off, and you need a home. This one is going to need a great deal more work, and I'm betting after today it will need a little more." He pulled to a stop in front of the pack house. "Jodie is going to need you after this. Her father isn't just ill, and we both know it. If he makes it through the night, it will be a miracle. She may not like her family overly much, but they're all she has."

"I hate this." Phil didn't say anything, but only nodded at him. "All right. Get them out and we'll go from there. My hands are tied until my test results come back, so maybe after the Fields get out I can start on the house."

"Oh, don't you worry about them. They'll be gone in the morning."

Reid didn't think about what he'd meant by that. If they were gone in the morning, so much the better. He'd not think about if they were gone as in moved out or gone as in never

45

heard from or seen again.

When he got out of the car at the house, he could hear arguing all the way to where they were standing. He looked at Phil.

"I believe your mate is upset about something." Reid nodded and moved toward the front porch. "Do you suppose she'll learn that CJ is a good deal stronger than her and simply listen?"

"Nope. And I wouldn't be so sure about her being stronger. The last time I saw her she was pounding her brothers against the wall without so much as breathing hard." Phil laughed as they entered the house. "But if you tell CJ that, I'll hunt you down."

Holly was sitting on the chair, watching the other two women. Nancy walked in with two glasses of tea just as Reid took one of the other seats and laughed when he realized that Holly and Nancy were watching them for entertainment value. He watched Jodie as she moved back from CJ.

"You think you're all that, don't you. Well, I got news for you, missy, I'm much bigger and badder than you'll ever be." Reid watched Jodie stretch her neck as CJ continued. "You'll do as you're told, or so help me, I'll tie you to the bed and have Reid sit on you."

CJ started forward, but stopped suddenly. Reid realized in that second that Jodie was holding her somehow. He started to stand up when he felt something, or in this case someone, pin him against the wall.

"I'm sick to death of telling you that I don't need, don't want, nor do I particular care for, your kind of help. I've been on my own, fending for myself long enough to know that the only person I trust is me." CJ sat down in the chair next to him but didn't move. "Now you're going to sit here like a good alpha until I get out of this bedlam. And then you're going to leave me the fuck alone. Do I make myself perfectly clear?"

"That's enough." Phil's mom materialized in the room just as Jodie turned to leave. "Sit down right now."

Jodie was in pain, he could see that from where he was, but there wasn't anything he could do about it at the moment. Trying to ignore a compulsion as strong as Hope Campbell could use had to hurt her. Hope was an old and powerful vampire. But Jodie did fight her until Hope staggered back.

"Oh my." Jodie moved toward the door and out. She wasn't steady on her feet, but she did make it. When he heard the bike start up and move down the drive, he felt his body relax by degrees. He looked at Hope when she said his name.

"She's not a just a shifter…you know that, right?" Reid nodded, not fully understanding what was going on, but knew she was right. "She's not going to be easy to get to love you, but when she does, it's going to be the forever kind of love. You understand what I mean?"

"No. I'm not entirely sure, but she did just knock you on your ass and was able to brush off CJ." Hope grinned at him as he continued. "Why on earth do you find that funny?"

"Because, my dear boy, you've met a woman who can kick my ass. Not many, only a handful at best, can do that." Hope stood up and touched his cheek. "Claim her soon, son; if you don't, then she'll leave and you'll never find her. She'll make sure you don't."

47

CHAPTER 5

Jodie sat on the bed and took deep breaths. It was supposed to calm her, but all it did was bring the scent of the wolf into her nose. She finally gave up and stripped down. A shower was what she needed. She turned the tap as hot as it would go before stepping under the spray.

He was simply too much for her. Washing her hair, she thought about the way he'd pressed her against him and wondered about doing more with the big man. Reid was entirely too much for any one woman to want to handle, and she was sure others would agree with her. And she was not going to see if she could. Not now, and not ever.

Scrubbing her body until it burned, she let the water spray over her until she felt she could get out without tensing up again. The vampire had scared her, not because she'd had to work so hard to ignore the compulsion, but because she was pretty sure she'd figured out what she was.

Jodie wrapped the towel around her body and moved into the bedroom. She wasn't really frightened by the man standing there, but she didn't turn her back on him either. When he said her name, she turned and glared.

"You said we were finished. You said if I left this time,

you would wash your hands of me and I'd be free. I held up my end of the bargain, so you should too." He sat down on nothing that was in this room and asked her to do the same. "No. You should leave before they know you're here."

"They won't find me. I missed you." She rolled her eyes at him and moved around the room to find something to wear that didn't smell of Reid. "I've some news for you. If you come back for a few days, I'll give it to you. And you have to finish your training. You've only one more thing to complete."

"It's no longer important to me, and I don't want it bad enough to go back." She watched him as she pulled her panties up under the towel, then her pants. Tugging a shirt over her and the towel, she pulled it from under the shirt and stood there.

He'd never been interested in her sexually. And even though he was a vampire, he'd never bitten her either. They'd been...friends, she supposed, for a while until he'd tried to make her do something she swore she'd never do.

"The man who claims to be your mate, what do you know of him?" She didn't answer as she reached for some socks to put on. "He's going to be a powerful doctor, healing those that would die without his help. You'll need to allow him to claim you, or it will never happen."

"I don't want to be claimed. You of all people should know that." He nodded and looked sad. "Why do you care if a wolf is a doctor and whether or not I get claimed by him or not?"

"No reason." He moved around the room, not seeing what was there. She knew this because he'd walked through a chair, and now stood in the middle of a table. "I should like to give you a gift."

"You've given me enough, thanks." With her shoes on, she went to get her wallet and bag. She was going to go out and find someplace that would serve her a thick steak and the biggest baked potato she'd ever seen. "Are you coming with me or staying here?"

"I'll come." She moved to the door and locked it after going out of it. When he appeared beside her, she didn't say anything to him, as there were two people in the hall with her. No one but her could see him, and she liked that just fine. But he could talk to her.

When they all entered the elevator, she had to look away when he was standing where the woman was. Not just where she was, but it looked like he wore her as a suit. When the couple got out, she moved out of the hotel so thcy could no longer hear her.

"Are you going to tell me the real reason you're here or not?" They were on a busy street now, and she pulled out her ear piece and stuck it in her ear. It didn't work, of course. She didn't own a cell phone, but it made her look less crazy when she spoke to him.

"I've come to ask you about the vampire I felt touching you today. She is very powerful, and I think I know her." Jodie held a door open at the deli she was going to have dinner at while a woman and her child walked out. "What's her name? And did you know that she's full blooded?"

"No, why would I know that? I don't even know your name, much less hers. All I've ever known about you is the little snippets you've granted me." He nodded and moved to the table she was planning to sit at. She knew that he'd keep the others away so that she'd have a seat where they could talk when she got her food. He'd done it for her before.

"I've given you a great deal, or tried to. You never wanted anything from me." She sat down when he sighed heavily. "I've tried and tried, but all you wanted was training."

"That's all you said you'd give me. I can't help it if you changed your mind later. And I've tried to pay you for it, but you refused." She looked at the sandwich, no longer hungry.

"You should eat. You'll need your strength in the coming days." She glared at him. "You can see it too if you wish. Just touch your mate of your own free will and you'll know it too."

"I told you that part of what I am is off limits to everyone." She picked up the sandwich, knowing that he was guiding her to eat it, and finished it off. It was that or fight him, and she didn't have the strength after the fight today.

"Tell me your name, all of it." She glanced at him as he spoke. "I'll tell you mine if you tell me yours."

"You told me never to give anyone my name. I've even worked to erase it from my family's mind. Why would you give it to me now?" He moved to the other side of the room and brought something back with him. Whatever it was, she would be able to see it but not touch it. He laid the book in front of her.

"I'm sending this to you tomorrow. Show it to the vampire from today. You do that and I'll finish your training." She shook her head, and he nodded. "You have to do it. She already knows that you and I are together. Mistress Vampire is very strong and can give me what I need."

"And what is that?" The book started to turn pages, and she could see glimpses of some of the pages. Blood on one page covered almost the entire thing…a pendent on another page that she'd seen before, but knew that the man no longer wore when she was around. When the pages stopped moving, she looked down at the page, then up at him.

"Is it her?" She nodded, and the pages turned again. "This man, have you seen him as well?"

The man looked like Phil the lawyer, but not quite. He had the same strong features, but the man in the drawing looked less handsome and more…she supposed pretty would be a good word. She shook her head, staring at the man on the page.

"It is her mate. His name I do not know either, but I've seen him a great many times over the centuries with the woman." The book disappeared, and he sat down. "The book needs to be given to her and only her. Will you do this for me?"

"Why?" He smiled at her, and she felt his sadness. "You want this from me, what do I get in return?"

He nodded. He'd trained her well. Never give anything without a fair exchange. When he nodded, she felt the air around her tighten, and suddenly he was sitting next to her, in the flesh this time. Glancing around the room, she could see that not one person noticed him, and she'd bet that if asked they'd never seen her either.

His touch to her forehead made her cry out. Memories flooded her mind, and she felt as if they spilled from her nose and ears. He handed her a napkin, and she dapped at the blood there and looked at him as he faded out.

"Give it to her and only her for me. Then in two days' time, I'll come to you. She'll… if she asks you to summon me, tell her that you will. Call for me."

"I don't know your name." His laughter faded with him, and she stood up. "What's your fucking name?"

"You've known it as long as you've known me." She sat there for an hour trying to think when she'd ever known his name. Not one time did he ever say it in all the five years she was his apprentice. Jodie left the deli in a huff. She had a good mind to burn the fucking book when it got there.

~~~

Austin didn't want to be impressed by the girl, but he was. She didn't squirm like most people did when they sat in his office, but she sat there not moving at all. He'd bet that she was asleep but for the fact that she blinked occasionally.

"Hope said she'd be here soon." Jodie nodded. "Would you like to talk about your relationship with Reid?"

"We don't have one." That didn't go over as well as he'd hoped. He'd hoped for her to ask him why she was his mate or at least be pissy. This cold woman before him made him nervous as hell. When someone knocked at his door, he was so relieved that he found himself hoping for Reid, but when Hope stepped into the room with Phil, he knew this wasn't going to go as well as he'd thought.

"I have a book for you." Phil reached for it and Jodie snatched it back. "I said I have one for her, not you. I was told to give it to her and only to her."

"By who?" Jodie only stared at Hope and she right back at her. He'd heard about the other day when Jodie had tossed her off. Austin wanted to be pissed about what she'd done to CJ, but she'd told him it was her fault. He doubted it was entirely her fault but wouldn't bring it up, as she'd asked him not to.

"He said that you'd know when you received the book. Do you want it or not?" Hope stepped to Jodie but didn't touch her. She did, however, lean in and sniff her. When she took a step back, Hope looked pale.

"Yes, I'll take…Christ, you know him." Hope took the book and stiffened slightly. Phil went to her side, and then when she was seated, he moved to Jodie. Before Austin could move to intercept him, he was flying back against the wall and Phil was a foot off the ground without anyone touching him.

"Please, let them go. They won't harm you. I promise you." Austin stood up, but he made no move toward either woman as Hope pleaded with Jodie. Phil was still hanging there, and Hope begged again. He was put down, but he didn't move back.

"He said I was to give it to you and you'd understand. Do you?" Hope nodded at Jodie and she leaned over to pick up her bag. "Good, then I'm finished here."

She moved to the door, but before she got more than a foot from it, Hope spoke again. "You have the power to heal him, but you won't. You also had the power to kill me yesterday, but you didn't do that either. Would you mind telling me why?"

Jodie stood there for several seconds. Austin wasn't sure she was going to answer her, but when she did so without turning, he wondered about that as well.

"To harm is to have it returned tenfold. To kill is to have

it returned by a dozen times a dozen. To love is to have it returned without numbers." Jodie turned her head slightly to look at Hope. "To heal him would not change the outcome."

"No, but he is your father." Jodie shook her head. "He's not your sire? Do you know who is?"

"I do." Jodie was out the door before any of them could question her further. When they heard the big bike start and the sound move away, Austin sat down at his desk and put his head in his hands.

"What the hell was that?" He looked at Hope. "You know what she is, and I'm betting it's not as simple as a shifter, is it?"

"No, she's not a simple shifter. At least she's not anymore. Someone has trained her on the things she was more than likely born with and has enhanced them for her. I wouldn't doubt that she's aware of them, but she might not know just how powerful she really is." Hope looked at the book that Jodie had given her and ran her fingers over the cover reverently. "She has given me a great deal with this book. Did she tell you what it was?"

"No. She came here telling me that she needed to speak to you. She said that since it was my territory and that she was a shifter that all beasts that she used had to be present when the exchange was made. Mom said that, while that's partly true, all that had to be here was another person. I don't know why she asked for Phil too."

"Because he's a vampire in this area that she has to answer to. If the shit hit the fan, as I believe you younger people like to say, she wanted everyone to know that she'd given me the book and I accepted it."

"It's that important?" Hope nodded at Phil's question. "What is it, Mom? What's in that book that would have her come here to give just to you?"

"It's the *Book of Life*. The first book that we brought here when we came here." She opened the first page and showed them the names. "So many of these people are gone now, and there are so many that their lives were lost because of this book."

"They wrote down the names of all the vampires that came here? That's just nuts." Austin flushed when he realized that he himself had a similar book with names and apologized to them both. "The woman scares me if you want to know the truth."

"And well she should. If the man I think trained her did it, she's probably the most powerful being alive next to him. He would...I'm thinking that now that he's given up the book, he plans to give her whatever else she doesn't have, and she'll be unstoppable."

"Why her?" Austin looked up to see Reid standing in the doorway. "I've heard what you said, but why her? She have something he wants?"

"No. I would think that she has all he could ever give her, and she him. He has only touched her once, I think. And her training would have been years and years." Hope frowned. "But that can't be either. She's so young, in her mid-twenties I would think. The kind of training she's had—" She stopped talking and opened the book. "Do you know this man? Any of you?"

No one did, and that seemed to upset her more. When asked who he was, she said she couldn't remember. Phil took the book from her, and it snapped shut, and no matter how much he tried, he couldn't get it to open. Hope looked at Reid.

"Open it." He backed from it. "Your mate gave it to me, so you should be able to open it. Try."

"I don't think I want to." Austin started to tell him to when Reid looked at Hope. "She has a reason for giving it to you, and if she wants me to open it, I'll wait for her to ask. Otherwise, I don't think I should."

Hope nodded and held the book to her breast. "I must go now, but I'll return. I'm betting that whoever gave her the book will come to her soon, and if I were you, I'd try my best to be there when he comes. You might not get the chance to meet him again."

Hope disappeared, and Reid sat down. He looked worried, not that Austin blamed him. Phil cleared his throat and changed the subject.

"The squatters have moved out." He grinned, and Austin thought that whatever he'd done must have been fun for the vampire. "Holly helped me. She said it was the most fun she'd had in a while."

"What did you do?" Austin laughed when Reid asked suspiciously, "You didn't kill them did you? Are they going to haunt me for the rest of my life?"

"No, good heavens no. But they won't be back. Especially the female. And if you should be worried about anyone, it should be her. She's a little scary when she wants to be." Phil sobered as he pulled an envelope out of his pocket. "But I'm afraid the damage is extensive. They will be sued, of course, but they have no money, so it will be a loss."

The pictures were five by sevens, but they were detailed enough that Austin could see it would be months before he'd be able to move in. Austin decided that he'd have the crew go over in the morning and get a start. Especially on the kitchen, where it looked like they'd taken a chainsaw to the room and the appliances.

"I guess we'll have to think of somewhere else for Jodie and I to stay until this is finished." Reid looked at Phil when he nodded. "I guess I'll have to use that money now. Can you make arrangements to have an account opened up that I can get to?"

"Already done. And I've taken the liberty of adding Jodie's name to the account too, if that's all right with you." Reid nodded, but he didn't look happy. The house was his dream, and now this.

CHAPTER 6

Reid sat as still as he could. He'd been summoned there early this morning by a phone call that had told him where to come and what time, but nothing else. He'd agreed before he'd thought to figure out why. Now he was sitting in this deli waiting for someone to come in. He hoped. For all he knew he was there to be killed. Then he saw her.

Jodie slid her leg over the bike and took off her helmet as she stood up. Her hair was in a tangled bun, and when she took the rubber band out and let it tumble, he whimpered before he could catch himself. There was a soft laugh next to him that had him turn.

"She's very lovely, isn't she?" The man leaned back and smiled. "You're the mate."

Reid looked at the man, trying to figure out what he was seeing that was wrong. "You're not here."

"No. Very good, wolf." Reid felt as if he was ten years old and had gotten the answer correct in class. "She's not going to be happy that I invited you here. But it is important that you both are."

"You called me." The man nodded. "Why would you do that if you knew it was going to make her mad?"

"She will understand, both of you will in a few moments. She is very strong." Reid told him he'd gotten that. "She had bested you then?"

"No, her brothers. They're not going to live long if they hurt her again." When she entered the deli, he stood up. She started to back away when the man sitting next to him stood up as well. She moved toward the table and sat down. A sandwich appeared before them both.

"Why are you forever trying to get me to eat?" She shoved the plate away. "What is he doing here?"

"*He* is right here and can answer for himself." The man interrupted them both and asked about the book.

"She took it as you knew she would. And you lied to me. I do not know who you are. I have been wracking my brain trying to figure it out and you've never told me." Jodie looked at him. "Do you know him?"

"No." Reid didn't mention that he'd seen his picture in the book that Jodie had given Hope, but the man seemed to know. When he winked at him, Reid had the most overwhelming feeling of friendship. The man nodded at him.

"I need to give you the rest of your training. You've earned it." He seemed to solidify for a moment then faded again. "I think we should do this in a more private setting."

The rush of air and the feeling of movement was all the warning he got before he was sitting in a living room…his living room as a matter of fact. But this one was clean of all the mess the squatters had left him, and the furniture was new. He wanted the room to look like this someday, but he was far from this.

"It is now." He looked at the man who walked around

the room touching things. "I've given it to you as a gift. You may consider it a wedding gift."

Reid looked at Jodie to see what her reaction was and noticed that she lay sleeping on the end of the couch. Moving to her, Reid checked her pulse and looked at the man.

"Yes, I did this to her." He sat down. "I would like a word before I wake her. She will be most displeased with us, I think. She does not trust me even though I have no reason at all to harm her. Nor should I ever want to."

Reid could see that. She didn't really seem to trust anyone. When the man sat down and smiled at him, Reid said the first thing that popped into his head.

"You're her father." The man clapped his hands and smiled. "Christ, and she doesn't know that."

"No, she doesn't. She thinks it is another man, not the one that lay dying in the clinic, but one that is strong but not a very good man. Neither am I, but I would never hurt her for what she is. He would...I think he would take and take from her until she has nothing more to give. Then he would take just enough more to kill her."

"And what do you want from her?" He sat back on the seat and they both looked at her. "You do, don't you, want something from her?"

"Happiness?" Reid shook his head as he looked back at the man. "I do, but that's not what I need from her. She will be all that I have left to leave behind. The two of you. I should like to give it to her, but I fear...."

"You fear what?" Reid asked when he didn't finish. He looked pensive and nervous. Reid watched him as he stood up to pace, and when he stopped suddenly and looked at

63

Jodie, he knew without looking that she was awake. And she looked pissed.

"Where am I?" She stood up and then sat down. "You've done that stupid moving fast thing again, haven't you? How many times have I told you not to…? What's happened?"

The abrupt change of subject startled him but didn't bother the man as he smiled and answered her. "Nothing has happened, my dear. But your mate and I have been discussing your finer qualities."

"Finer my ass." He laughed. "I did what you asked. Now finish this. You said I'd be trained on the last thing, whatever that is, and now give it to me."

"You'll not like it." She shook her head and told him to just do it. "You must feed from your young mate here."

Reid wasn't sure which of them was more shocked, her or him, but she was a good deal more vocal about it. He'd never heard a more colorful string of curse words in his life. And the man simply let her.

"Who the hell are you?" The question slipped out before he could think. Both of them looked at him before Jodie looked at the man. "I don't know what to call you, and I'm pretty sure I should have something before I let her bite me."

"I'm not biting you." She stood up to pace and walked by them both twice before she turned on the vampire. "What is this really about? You know that I'll never feed from anyone. First, it's not necessary, and second, I simply won't do it."

"Then you'll never know." She stomped past him to the doorway and started over the threshold when he spoke again. "Do you not really care to be whole, Jolene?"

She turned back slowly. Even from the distance of his room he could see that she was pissed. Jodie was really a Jolene? He wondered if her last name was even Turner. Reid stood up when she moved toward the man, and when he didn't move, Reid thought he wanted her to hurt him.

"You fucking prick. You said to me about four million times, 'don't tell anyone your real name.' Having that is something akin to giving them a taste of your blood." He still hadn't moved. "Stand up."

"Why?" Reid wanted to know too and was afraid the answer wasn't going to be good.

"Because I want to knock you on your ass." Reid started to laugh but realized she wasn't kidding. Before he could tell her that wasn't such a good idea, the man stood up.

"Tristan Elden." He frowned, and Jodie did as well. "You wanted to know my name. Well, it's Tristan Elden."

"Now you tell me." Tristan nodded. "Why now? What possible reason could you have for telling me now?"

"You need him more than you need me." Jodie looked at Reid and shook her head before looking at Tristan again. "You've no desire to die, do you, Jolene? You have unfinished business, and he will help you accomplish it. If you don't take him, you'll die."

"You're lying." She nodded when he shook his head. "You would do or say anything that would get me to do what you want me—"

"Ask me the rest. I told you if I ever felt you were ready for it all, I'd give it to you. Ask me now." Jodie backed up and put her hands behind her back. "If you don't ask, how will you know the truth?"

65

"I don't want it anymore." Jodie looked at him. "This has gone on long enough. I want you to take me back to the hotel, and let's forget the whole thing. I don't...I'm going to have to leave soon anyway."

"You can't leave. I need you." Reid walked toward her slowly. She reminded him of a beaten animal and she would tear your hand off if you reached for her too quickly. "You know what he's telling you is true, don't you? If you don't take me as your mate, you'll die."

"Then I'll die."

~~~

Jodie walked out of the room this time. She wasn't going back either. They were both certifiable, and she was going to wait for her father to pass, sell the property to the highest bidder, and hope to Christ she never heard of this place again. She was standing in the front hallway when she stopped. She didn't need this or want it.

"Mother fuck." Moving back to the living room, she glared at Tristan. He was still sitting in the same place he'd been when she'd left, and Reid was standing near the unlit fireplace. "I want you to know that I fucking hate you both."

"Noted." Tristan sat there as if he had not a care in the world. "But you should also note that while you don't believe me, I do love you very much."

"Fuck off." She sat down and tried to ignore the wolf that moved with the grace of his beast and looked good enough to eat. When he sat beside her, she tried to move to the other side of the couch, but he simply pulled her back. Fuck this crap too. She needed answers, and now that Tristan Elden was willing to give them to her, she was going to ask them.

66

"Who are you to me?" He grinned like she had just given him the world. "And I don't want any bullshit answer that you're my Zen teacher and that I've been chosen for this great life."

"I'm your sire." She thought he'd say something like, "Just kidding," but since he'd never joked with her before, she wasn't surprised that he didn't. He just sat there staring at her, and she leaned back, right against Reid's hand. Before she could tell him to back the fuck off, she fired off her next question.

"Will I still be able to finish what I've started if I don't take Reid as my mate?" Tristan nodded, then shook his head. "Both answers won't work. One or the other."

"You'll finish what you've started, but you'll never live to see it to completion." He leaned forward and rested his elbows on his knees. "Without him, you'll only see that the… end, shall we call it, is accomplished, but nothing more."

"You mean that I'll be able to kill him, but I'll die too." He nodded. "But I win. He'll be dead and the rest will fall into place."

"No. It will eventually, but not in time." She glanced at Reid when he cleared his throat. Tristan explained some of it to him. "Jolene has a man that she wants to kill. And not just any man, but a mage. Do you know what they are?"

"I do. What did he do to her?" Jodie didn't want to be impressed that he didn't tell her no she wasn't going to, or worse yet tell her that she wasn't strong enough or some shit. "And why is it important that she bite me?"

"Jolene?" Tristan wanted her to tell Reid. She wanted to brain them both. Why the hell couldn't she have just simply

67

finished her training that didn't involve a mate and be done with it?

"Stop calling me that." She looked at Reid. "I have to bite you so that I can transfer all that I am to you and vice versa. Mostly it's for you to help me kick his ass, but I really don't want you there."

"But you need me." She didn't answer because that would be the same as admitting that she needed someone, and she didn't. Instead, she asked Tristan something else.

"Why didn't you tell me you were my father before now? And who is my mother?" She flushed when Reid winked at her. It was as if he was saying, "I know you changed the subject, but I'll get back to it soon."

"I didn't tell you before now because you would have been pissed off about it and not listened to me train you." He was right, but she wasn't going to tell him that. "As for your mother, she was a shifter like you, but you're so much… more."

"How did she end up with the Turners? I'm assuming that her mother is deceased." Tristan nodded but didn't answer him. "Do they know that she's not their sister? I'm assuming that the old man knows."

"He does. And no, the boys do not know. They believe that while their mother was a wolf and never turned their father, that is why she has the ability to shift into other animals. The older boy, Curt, was but a baby when she was found." Reid was suddenly holding a picture of a man and woman. He handed it to Jodie as Tristan continued. "The woman is my mate and your mother, Kelley. She lost her life trying to hide from men who didn't understand what she

68

was."

"And you? Where were you when this happened?" Reid could hear the anger is Jodie's voice and really couldn't blame her for it. "Aren't you supposed to protect her with your life?"

"I was beneath the earth dying. But I felt her death in my heart. It took me nearly all your life to bring myself from my grave to find you. I had no idea that you existed until then." Tristan got up to pace as he continued. "The mage you seek, he's the one that murdered her. He is also the reason that I was where I was when she died. He wanted her, you see, and would stop at nothing to have her. It's why he did to you what he did. He wishes to have you in her place."

"What did he do?" Tristan continued to pace and didn't answer Reid. So he got up and went to Jodie. "What did the mage do to you?"

Instead of answering him, she lifted her sleeves on her shirt. It wasn't until then that he realized that she always wore long sleeves, even in her tee-shirts. When she held her arms out to him, he could see the scars there.

"He tried to kill me. I was seventeen and had been on my own for only about a month when he found me. I didn't have any idea how to fight him, or for that matter how to even save myself. But he…I hurt him somehow, and that's all that saved me." Reid pulled her wrists to his mouth and kissed the wide claw marks there. Dozens of them ran deeply along her wrists up to her elbows. He asked her if there were more. When she nodded and turned, he lifted her shirt up to expose her back.

It looked as if she'd gone a few rounds with a tiger.

Claw marks ran up and down as well as crossways across her back. Most of them were so deep they'd been stitched closed, the pucker marks evident among them. He lifted the shirt higher and found marks along her neck to her throat and up into her hairline. Reid wanted to pull her into his arms and hold her, but she stepped away before he could.

"Are they all over your body?" She nodded as she walked to the other side of the room and sat down. "How long were you in the hospital?"

"Three months. They told me I was lucky to be alive." Her laughter was bitter and manic sounding. "I wish I would have given up some days instead of setting out to prove them wrong."

"I found her there, in the hospital." Reid looked at Tristan, who was now seated again. "She was nearly healed by then, and since she wouldn't take even a sip of my blood, I couldn't heal her."

"So you trained her instead." Tristan nodded at him. "And you knew when you took her under your wing that the same mage that hurt your mate is the one that hurt your daughter."

"No. I didn't know who had hurt her until a few years later. Jolene had a horrific nightmare one night during our time together. I only meant to sooth her, but I found her memories of the monster who did that to her. It was then that I decided to give her everything." Tristan seemed to come to a decision as he continued. "You know that when he finds her, and I've no doubt that he's still looking, that he'll stop at nothing this time to kill her. She's much more powerful than she'd been as a child."

"He'll kill her for her own powers. They'll come to him when he kills her." Tristan smiled sadly and nodded. "He won't get the chance."

Reid pulled her up from the couch and into his body. She was stiff yet didn't fight him. When he buried her face into his throat, she licked him but nothing more. Tristan cleared his throat.

"You do know that's not what I meant when I said she needs to drink from you." It took Reid a few seconds to realize what he'd meant and flushed. "Yes, you'll need to mate and bond for it to be finished."

Jodie pulled from him. "It's not going to happen. I'll take my chances with the mage, and if I die, then I do."

She backed away from him and turned to the door. He started after her when she stopped and held up her hand. Reid was frozen in place. Looking at Tristan, he could see that she held him as well, and both of them watched as she moved across the room and disappeared. They were both released as soon as she was gone.

"I wish now I'd not trained her on that trick." Reid wished Tristan hadn't either. Sitting down on the couch, he tried to think what to do now. That's when Tristan lifted his head up.

"She will die if you don't bond with her." Reid nodded, but his hands were tied since she didn't give him permission. "You need only to make her aware of what you plan to do to her. I'm sure you can be quite inventive if you set your mind to it."

When Tristan disappeared a few seconds later, Reid still had no idea what he'd meant. Standing up, he walked out of the living room and into the kitchen, almost afraid to see what damage had been done in there. He was shocked to see that this room, like the living room, was set to rights as well. Reid moved throughout the house and found that the entire house was now cleaned up as well as furnished.

Ending up in the master bedroom, he sat in one of the beautiful wing chairs near the fireplace. He was closing his eyes when a thought suddenly popped into his head. Smiling, he sat up.

"Now all I have to do is nip a little blood from her and I can do it." Sending her images of them together would either drive her over the edge or make her want to murder him. Either way, he was going to have some fun.

CHAPTER 7

Ethan Randolph sat quietly in his room. There was no furniture with the exception of a pad on the floor, and no windows. The walls had been painted with the blood of his victims, and under that was black magic. It was his own place to rest and to feel.

She was out there, the girl that had nearly killed him. And he was going to find her if it was the last thing he did. Smiling, Ethan reached deeper into the earth to see where she might have tread, but found only traces of her, not enough for him to actually find where she was now. He would find her soon. He had to.

The girl was stronger than she'd been as a teenager, but she'd never be strong enough to harm him again. He felt the scars she'd given him and the one wound that had yet to heal pull when he moved. She'd pay for those as well.

"I should have searched harder when I killed your mother and father. I would have had you long before now." Ethan smiled again, his fangs stretching below his lip as he thought of her mother. "Tasty."

She'd been a morsel he'd not been able to resist. Killing her mate had been incredibly easy, and he'd thought that she'd be easy as well, but she'd been like a bear with a cub. Ethan supposed now that he thought about it, she'd been just that. Protecting her cub would have been what drove her. And Kelley Elden had been a fighter.

Finding her after so long had been a miracle. Ethan hadn't really been looking very hard, he'd admit to himself now, but he'd been looking. She'd been powerful for a wolf, more than he'd ever thought, and her taste still lingered in his mouth when he wanted something to savor. But it hadn't been nearly enough. But now there was her child.

Ethan knew that he'd only found the girl by chance. She'd been coming out of a fast food restaurant when he'd been walking by it. Her scent had nearly had him take her then, but there were too many witnesses, and he was a little more cautious back then. Now he would simply have taken her and damn the others.

But he'd watched and listened, and finding her alone had been easy if not exciting. She'd been a good deal more than he thought she'd be for one so young. And she fought back with the savagery of a cornered animal. Which he supposed she was.

He'd gotten the jump on her, of course, but he'd never had the upper hand. She'd torn into him, shifting fast and attacking him as if she'd thought she had a chance of surviving. Ethan had been so terrified when she tore into his back that he'd allowed her to get to his throat. And when she'd torn into him, even though he knew she was close to dying, he had to leave her. It had taken him nearly a month to be able to move his head without pain from what she'd done to him, and longer to find someone to bleed dry for their magic. By then she had disappeared. That was over five years ago and he'd not been able to find her since.

Ethan knew that she lived. He could feel her heart beating from the little blood he'd managed to taste from her. It hadn't been enough to do much more than help him search for her, but enough that he knew she still lived.

And find her he would.

Moving to the upper levels of his home, Ethan moved through the house as quietly as the wind. He had no desire to talk with anyone in the house. And his servants knew better than to disturb him unless it was an emergency. Which was why when someone knocked on his door he'd been so startled that it had taken him several seconds to bid them enter.

"Master, there is a gentleman here to see you. He says you and he have an arrangement." Ethan nodded at his man servant. "Very good, sir. I will bring him to you directly."

He'd hired an investigator several months ago. And just last night he'd asked the man to come to the house. It was time to tell him that his services were no longer needed. As soon as he walked in the room however, Ethan knew that he'd finally found something.

"You told me once that there was a family by the name of Turner that had housed the girl's mother. Well, I think the girl showed up there last week." The man handed him a blurred picture of a person on a motorcycle. "I know this isn't the best picture in the world, but—"

"You are correct. For all I know this could be you on this thing." Ethan knew that it wasn't because this person was small while the man sitting across from him was a big as three of the biker. "If this is all that you have, I'm afraid that I have no more use—"

"She's a shifter." Ethan nodded for him to continue. "I've seen her shift into a hawk as well as a wolf. A big fucking wolf too. One of the others, a male that lives in the house, is a wolf as well, but nothing much to worry about. But the girl?" He pulled out another picture and handed it to him.

This one was of a man facing the camera and a woman with her back to it. The long dark hair seemed to be black, but the picture was of a substandard quality so it was difficult to tell. But the man standing next to them had his heart start to beat hard in his chest.

"Where was this taken?" The man took a step back, and Ethan felt his beasts roar at him. Trying for a calmer tone, he asked him again. He could tell that the man was frightened of him and any other time would have been thrilled by it, but not now.

"A little town in Ohio. I think…." He looked at his notes with a trembling hand. "Nashport. It's a deli called *Get Fresh With Me.* I've seen her in there several times, but never with these two men before. Should I find out who they are?"

"No. I will." He stood up and smiled when the man flinched. "While I would love to simply play with you, I have more pressing items on my agenda. Perhaps another time."

The man nodded, and Ethan had a feeling he'd never hear from him again. Not even to send a bill. Which suited him fine. Ethan would have killed him over it. This way the man got to live a little longer.

Ethan waited until he had his mind under control before

he used some of his considerable magic to will himself to Nashport, Ohio. It wasn't as difficult as it had been when he'd first tangled with the girl, but he was slightly weak from it. He was standing in front of the smallish deli with the bright windows seconds later, and something occurred to him. He should have asked the man what the girl's name was.

Moving slowly so as not to draw attention to himself, he found a hotel not far from where the deli was. There were people going in and out all the time, the doors barely closing before it opened again to bring customers in or to spill them out again. He'd gotten a room that overlooked the street and sat a chair in front of the window to watch. Even if he didn't know what she looked like or her name, he did know the man. Tristan Elden was going to lead him right to his daughter. Glancing down at the paper that had come with the room, he was startled to see the name he'd heard from the investigator. Turner.

Curtis Turner was dead. Not that Ethan knew who he was or if he was the one that the investigator had been talking about, but it was something to look into. Seeing that the funeral was at graveside in the morning, Ethan decided that he'd go because he knew it had to be one and the same. He did wonder what this man was to her, but decided that he honestly didn't care. So long as he found her, he was going to be very happy.

~~~

Jodie sat in the hotel room with the phone still in her hand. When the noise that it was making indicating that it was a dead line finally registered in her mind, she set it gently in the cradle. It was done. The realtor had a buyer for the property. All she had to do was meet him at the bank in the morning and it would be over. There would be no more ties to this town.

Moving to the bed, she lay down and closed her eyes. She wasn't tired, but she was overwhelmed. There was simply too much going on right now for her to be anything but terrified. When she'd been to see Curtis three days ago, she'd gotten into a fight with Mike and had been knocked around again. Lucky, or not so lucky for her brother, Reid had been there to pull him off her. She smiled when she thought of the way he'd paced in front of her while she held an ice pack to her head.

"You do know that you're twice the man he is, right?" She nodded once and had to stop because it made her slightly ill. "Why the fuck aren't you trying to fight back?"

"I can't. It's part of the rules that I signed off on when I became an apprentice to Tristan." She refused to call him Dad or even Father. Hell, she wasn't sure that calling him by his first name made her feel all warm and fuzzy. "If I harm or kill someone of my blood, I'm doomed to be hurt too."

"But he's not your blood." She'd thought of that too, but it was simply a matter of splitting hairs. He was as close to being her brother as anyone else, and it might turn back on her.

"His intent was to hurt me, not kill me. When he tries that, I can fuck him up." She had shrugged at him, and he stepped too close to her. "Back off, buddy. You're not related to me by proxy or anything else, and I will hurt your ass."

But all he did was taste her again. His tongue moved

down along her skin until she felt it all the way to her core. He knew it too, and when he nuzzled her neck, it was everything she could do not to beg him to take her. So when he stepped back from her, she did whimper aloud.

"You're going to be mine soon." She shook her head at him, and he smiled. "Oh but you will be. Soon you'll be begging me to take you, and I will be more than glad to do so."

When he'd stepped out of the room she'd been in, Jodie had to take several deep breaths to get her heart under control. Then she had to keep telling herself that going after the big wolf wasn't an option. She had something to do, and sleeping with him wasn't going to get her any closer to her goal. That hadn't gone over any better yesterday than it had the five or six hundred times she'd tried to tell herself that last night and today. The man was driving her over the edge of sanity.

Jodie opened her eyes when she felt someone touch her. As tightly as she held her body, she was surprised when she felt a whisper of a touch over her arm. Looking around the room, she couldn't see anyone but knew that someone was here. The second time someone touched her, it was along her ribs, and she nearly cried out when the touch moved over her breast.

Sitting up, she turned on the light to see that the room was devoid of anyone but her. Closing her eyes, she reached into the room to see if someone was there that had shadowed themselves, but found no one. That's when she felt her nipple being teased.

"Don't." The sound of her own voice startled her.

Looking around the room, she nearly cried out again when she felt someone brush across her lips. She knew who it was immediately.

Reid had somehow gotten into her mind. Before she could block him out, he sent her image after image of him and her together. And the more he flashed before her closed eyes, the more erotic they got, until he was taking her against the wall and her legs wrapped around him.

"Why are you doing this?" He didn't answer, but she could feel his need. *"Stop this right now or so help me, I'll make you regret it."*

"Come for me." She felt her body burn to do just what he wanted. *"Better yet, come here and let me taste you when you come."*

Her legs spread all on their own when she felt him touching her clit. She was burning for him now, his magical touch not nearly enough. Over and over he moved above her, touching but not where she needed him to be, sliding his fingers over her only enough to make her want more. Relief wasn't going to come if he wasn't with her in the flesh.

His mouth touched her breasts. Her nipples hardened so tightly that they ached. Rubbing her hands over them, trying to alleviate the need, she only made it worse, her body humming with need.

"Why are you doing this?" Again he didn't answer her, but he didn't stop either. Her entire body was poised on the edge of the cliff, and he was the only one with the power to push her over. Need rolled over her, and she was so close that she could almost taste it when he suddenly stopped.

Jodie laid there for several minutes. She wanted him to

continue doing what he'd been doing, but more than that, she needed him to finish her. When she reached for him, she met with only a block wall and couldn't beg him to do anything. Standing up, she began to pace the room, her body hurting for a completion she hadn't reached.

"I'll do it myself." Stripping down, she moved to the center of the bed and ran her fingers through her wet curls. Every time she touched her clit, she felt her body stir, but she knew that she'd find no relief. He'd brought her to this point, and now she was going to kill him for it. The more she flicked her fingers over her wet clit, the stronger her need became until it was no longer just need but a necessity. Jodie decided she was going to murder him when she saw him again. The phone ringing startled her enough that she cried out. Then she felt stupid for letting a man bring her to this point.

"Hello." Okay, she didn't need to take it out on the person at the other end, then revised that thought when she heard the laughter at the other end. She hated Phil almost as much as she did Reid right now.

"Are you all right, my dear? You sound frustrated." She might have thought that he knew something, but thought that he was simply stating a fact. "Now that Curtis is dead, we need to get together and see what you want to do with the sale of the property."

She started to tell him she had it under control when she thought about him knowing she'd sold it already. The phone call had only happened less than thirty minutes ago, and she knew that the realtor wouldn't have called him too.

"I haven't done anything with the property as yet. What

do you mean?" He laughed again in that sarcastic way that grated on her nerves. "Who called you?"

"The buyer. Austin has had his eye on this land for some time. He'd even offered Curtis a fair amount for it before you came in and paid off the taxes. Did you know that the land butts right up against his?" She didn't know that and told him so. "He's to meet you at the bank in the morning, and so you know, he's paid the asking price. That should put a nice deposit in your account."

The asking price was enough to put a deposit on a great many things, one of which was a house she'd had her heart set on since she'd been a child. It was not far from where she was now, but she knew that it was a pipe dream. Buying that house would put her close to her brothers, as well as the Force family.

"If I sign a waiver, can you complete the sale?" He told her no. "Why not? I thought that's what lawyers were for. Besides fucking up people's lives and robbing them blind."

He laughed. Phil was the strangest man she'd ever met and by far the weirdest lawyer. When he calmed down enough where she could speak to him again, he still chuckled at her as she continued.

"I don't understand you. Any of you people. Are you on drugs or something? I simply want to get this completed, make sure the fucking bastard is dead, and get on with my life."

She could almost hear his smile. "Does that include Reid? Will you allow him to be a part of your life now that you've settled this part of things?"

"I don't have room in my life for a mate. And if you

knew me better, you'd try to convince him that he's better off without me. I'm not a nice person, and I'm horribly… messed up. Not just my body but my head too. And my body is bad enough." She no longer even looked at herself in the mirror. It was bad enough that she had to see her arms. "The mage did a number on me before he got away. I'm not…I'm not whole anymore."

"What do you mean, Jodie? Not whole how?" She looked around the lovely room and didn't answer him. She had been injured, more than just her flesh but inside as well. Children were never going to be an option for her, and she knew that as a wolf, Reid would want plenty.

"Never mind. Curtis's funeral is set for tomorrow at ten. I'll be at the bank at noon. Will Mr. Force be able to make it?" She heard papers shuffle around and waited for Phil to answer.

"He can. I have his schedule here. He wants to also go over the house with you. He will want to know what you want from it." She thought he was kidding her. What the fuck would she want from that disgusting house? Then she realized that Austin had never been in it.

"Nothing. There is nothing in that house I want. When I left, I took what I wanted with me and that's it. He can do whatever he wants with the furniture too. For all I care, he can burn the place down." She felt tears threaten as she realized that she truly didn't have anything there. "I'll be at the bank at noon."

She put down the phone and lay back on the bed. Jodie was depressed now and didn't really understand why. When the phone rang again, she didn't answer it. Nor the next four times it rang. Finally, when it stopped, she closed her eyes and fell to sleep.

CHAPTER 8

Reid knew that going to her hotel was a mistake. But she wasn't answering the phone, and frankly, he was worried. She might be all tough and bad assed, but she was still his mate. The second time he had to knock on her door, he was ready to bust it in. When he heard her moving around, he still wasn't satisfied until she opened the door. Finally, when she did, he could only stare at her.

Christ, she looked good enough to eat. Her hair was tousled and laying down over her unfettered breasts. The tee-shirt she had on was tight, and her nipples were hard and peaked. The shirt hung just to the top of her panties that would make any man whimper, and she was his.

Not really thinking about what she might do to him, Reid pulled her to him and kissed her. Her arms wrapping around him was all the invitation he needed to lift her up and take her to the nearest hard surface.

The bed was there, and he wanted to lay her across it and feast on her as he'd imagined doing when he'd been in her mind, but he didn't go that way, but to the wall directly across from them. As soon as he had her pressed against it, he tore her shirt off her and took her breast into his mouth and suckled.

"Reid, please." He had no idea what she wanted but knew how to please her. When her fingers curled into his hair and pulled him away from his bounty, he had to catch himself from snarling at her.

"This doesn't change a thing." He didn't answer her but took her mouth again. When she lifted his head this time, he rocked into her hard enough to make the pictures on the wall bounce. Whether she wanted to believe him or not, it changed everything.

Lifting her up high enough to open his jeans, she licked his throat. He could almost feel her hunger to bite him, but she stopped just short of sinking her teeth into him. He wasn't worried. Before this night was over, she'd be his and he would be hers. When he'd freed his cock, he tore her panties off and sank her onto him.

Of all the things he'd thought of when he took her, it wasn't her being a virgin. When she screamed out in pain, Reid's wolf snarled as well. He didn't care for his human hurting his mate. Reid didn't much care for it either.

"I'm so sorry, baby. I didn't know." He held her to him, not moving for fear of hurting her more. When she moved, he groaned and held her still with his hands on her hips. "I don't want to hurt you anymore honey, but if you move again, I'm going to come."

Her breath fanned across his pounding pulse, and he had to think of anything other than her. When Jodie nipped at his ear, he rocked into her as gently as he could, but he knew that he'd hurt her again because she groaned.

"Again." He looked at her thinking he'd not heard her

correctly. "Do that again, only harder this time."

Reid felt sweat roll down his back and his shirt stick to him. When he rocked his hips into her, she didn't groan, but she moaned deep in her throat. Moving slowly, he moved inside her a little harder with each up and down stroke.

"You're killing me." She smiled at him, then threw back her head and moaned. "Christ, I want to bite you."

He licked at the pounding pulse at her throat and nipped hard enough to draw blood but not mark her. When her fingers tightened in his hair, he did it again until she was riding him with a wildness that took his breath away. He wanted her to mark him, not because of what Tristan had told them, but because the thought of her sinking her fangs into him had his cock jerk inside of her. She moaned his name as she tightened her legs around him.

Moving to the bed with her wrapped around him, he sat down. She was all around him, so rolling her to her back and settling between her legs was easy. Lifting her breast to his mouth, he bit down on her nipple and felt her tighten around his cock.

Reid rolled into her over and over, bringing her just to the point of coming then slowing again. When she growled at him, he nearly laughed but was afraid she'd kill him. Now that he had her here, he wasn't taking any chances with her stopping him. Reaching up to his throat, he morphed his fingers into a sharp nail and opened his vein. As soon as she covered the wound with her mouth and sucked the first time, Reid pounded into her.

"Come. Come for me, Jodie." She rolled him to his back, never taking her mouth from his vein, and sat up, bringing him with her. She straddled him, rode him as she sealed the wound.

"I'm hungry." His heart skipped several beats when what she said sank in. "When I feed from you, you're going to have to do the same from me."

"I don't…how do I do that?" Her wrist was pressed against his mouth, and he bit into her. When her fangs tore into his throat, Reid rolled her to her back and came deep inside of her as she screamed out her own release.

Stars dotted his vision, and he felt his world darken as he came twice more. When she lifted her head from his throat and howled, Reid joined her. Christ, she was his. And he knew for as long as he lived, if he lived after this, there would never be a more defining moment in his life than having his mate feed from him.

When he dropped onto her, she wrapped her arms around him and held him to her. Rolling to his back, he pulled her with him and settled her lax body over his. He could hear her heart pounding as hard as his was and had to smile. Good Christ, she was amazing.

"You cheated." He lifted her head to see what she meant. "You sent me all those thoughts and images to make me want you more."

"So you wanted me, huh?" She slapped him on the chest as she laid back down. "I'm sorry, but you've no idea how hard it was for me not to come here and follow through on some of those. And I could feel your need, too, and that didn't help."

He ran his fingers up and down her back, touching places where he knew she'd been scarred. Reid wasn't worried about how they looked on her. She was his, and as far as he could see, she was perfect. When she spoke again, he could feel her pain, and it hurt him in ways he'd never imagined it would.

"I don't want this. I know that it's much too late for that, but I don't want this. I've enough going on, terrible things that you'll get hurt from, that having a mate will be dangerous. Not just for you but for both of us." She rolled to her back, and he moved to his side to look at her. She really was perfect. "The mage, when he finds me or I find him, he's going to use whatever he can to try and make me not kill him."

"You think he'll use me against you?" She nodded. "That means a great deal to me, you know. The fact that he can use me and it would upset you."

"I'm not in love with you. I'm not even sure I like you most of the time. The sex was…it was great, but it doesn't change that I don't want a mate." Reid nodded, trying his best not to be hurt by the truthfulness of her words. He didn't love her either, but he did want her.

Toying with her nipple, he watched it pucker under his fingers. When she moaned, he leaned over and licked her until she moaned. Lifting his head, he looked down at her. She was by and far the most beautiful creature he'd ever seen.

"I have this house. It's too fucking big for me, and thanks to your father it's well furnished and has a top of the line security system in it. I'd like for you to come and stay with me tonight. I know you have another life, and I'd never do anything so stupid as to tell you that you have to quit whatever it was and stay here with me. Nor am I stupid enough to think even if I did say that to you, you'd do it." He took her nipple into his mouth again and suckled just the tip until she arched beneath him. Lifting his head, he looked at her again and saw hunger. "I'd very much like to take you back to the house and fuck you again and again until neither of us can move."

He watched her face, looking for anything that would tell him she wasn't going to do as he asked. If nothing else, something that told him that she was leaving him now. But she finally nodded.

"I have Curtis's funeral tomorrow. Will you go with me? I need to…I have to prove to myself that he's really dead and gone."

"What did he do to you?" She stared off into the room, and he didn't think she'd answer him, but when she did, he felt as if finding Curtis and tearing him apart wasn't ever going to be enough.

"He did everything to me."

~~~

The house was much bigger than she'd thought. The master suite was bigger than her entire hotel room, as well as having a bathroom any girl worth her salt would kill for. It alone was enough for her to want to stay with him. When he asked her if she wanted a bath, she nearly shoved him out of the room so she could fill the enormous tub to the top and soak for a week in it.

Turning on the taps, she started to strip down. But he stood behind her and pulled her shirt off her, taking the time to kiss her shoulders and spine. By the time he'd taken off her bra, she was wet, and it wasn't from the steam of the tub. He was that yummy.

"I want to wash you. All of you." She nodded, wondering why she'd ever thought bathing alone was a good idea. Helping her into the tub after he'd stripped all her clothing off, he moved in behind her until she was cupped in front of him, back to chest.

The large sponge was incredibly soft against her skin and the soap he used smelled of vanilla and peaches. By the time he'd washed both arms and was rubbing it up and down her leg, she was as limp as a wet noodle and hot enough to boil water.

"Randy is my brother. We were going to buy this house together and sell it in a few years. But he decided that he wanted to live alone in the city closer to where he would be working." She didn't understand family. Hers was fucked up, and she didn't have any interaction with others so had no idea how other families worked together. "He's right, I suppose, in saying that it's for a man with a family."

Her heart clinched, but she kept her mouth shut. They were only going to be a fling for a little while, she told herself. As soon as she found the mage and killed him, he'd be sickened by her and want her to move on. Trying to ignore the pain that thought caused her, she started to scoot to the other side of the tub, only to be stopped by him.

"You've seen my body. Are you grossed out by it?" Shaking his head, he lifted her leg again, kissed one particularly nasty looking scar, and smiled at her. "My entire body is messed up. Inside and out."

"You can't have children. I'm aware of that." She looked

91

at him, shocked. "Jodie, I'm a doctor. I can see the damage on your abdomen and know that to have been hurt that badly you would have had internal injuries as well."

"You can't have children by me." He shrugged and moved toward her. "You're a wolf. You want to have lots of children. I can't give them to you."

"There are other ways to have children. Not all parents who have them want them. And there are children everywhere that have no one to love them." He kissed her on her mouth and moved to where her shoulder met her neck. "I want to mark you."

His teeth were sharp as he sank them into her. He didn't hurt her, but she was ready for him to take her again. Moving her hand up his body, she found his cock and wrapped her fingers around him. Reid moaned but didn't lift his head from where he was.

He was thicker than she'd thought. Of course, when he'd taken her the first time, she'd thought he was at least a foot thick. But now that she was touching him, she could barely get her fingers to touch around his shaft. When he sat up in the water, resting on his knees, she could see his cock just beneath the water.

Her mouth watered to taste him. Jodie wasn't sure how to tell him this, but he seemed to understand. Moving to the edge of the tub, he sat down and opened his legs. Sliding toward him, she put her hands on his thighs and looked up at him.

"You've no idea how much I want to feel your mouth on me." She nodded, thinking she wanted it as much as he seemed to. "Take me into your mouth, baby. I want to feel you suck me."

She wasn't sure what she thought he'd taste like, but the paradise that filled her mouth was enough to make her come. Swirling her tongue around his thick crown, she tasted something salty on her tongue and lifted her head. There was a drop of something creamy white at his tip, and she licked it into her mouth. Christ, it was enough to make her come again.

"Again. Christ, suck me again." His voice moved over her body like his hands did, touching her everywhere and making her need leap to nearly overwhelming her. When his fingers curled into her hair and held her over him, she nearly cried out when he rocked his hips up and touched the back of her throat.

Reid took her hand and put it over his sack. His balls were heavy, and she found that they were incredibly hot. Cupping them in her hands, she heard him moan and knew that he was enjoying this as much as she was. When they started to tighten next to his body, she knew that he was close to coming. And she planned to drink everything he gave her.

Twice he tried to pull her away, and the second time he did it she tightened her fingers on his balls. His low growl had her reaching between her legs and touching her clit, because she knew he was ready to come. When the first splash of his semen slid down her throat, she pinched her clit and came with him. Before she could bask much in what had just happened, he pulled her up and nearly threw her over the edge of the tub. Pulling her ass to him, he growled low when she turned to see what he was doing.

"My turn." Reid sounded strained. His voice made

her want more from him, much more. When he slammed his cock deep into her, she cried out and screamed out her release. Then he bit into her shoulder.

"Come," he commanded her. "Again. Come again." She did as he'd said three more times before she felt him tear into her flesh with his teeth. Pulling his wrist to her mouth, she bit into him, drinking deeply from him even as he roared out his climax.

Breathing wasn't difficult, but it was labored. Her heart felt as if she'd run several miles and all of it up hill. Licking the wound closed at his wrist, she heard him chuckle as he did the same to her shoulder.

"And this was funny how?" Reid kissed her shoulder and pulled her down onto his lap in the cooling water. She let him hold her not because he held her tightly but because it felt good. Jodie snuggled into his neck and closed her eyes. "I have to go back to my hotel soon. I have my clothes there and some other things I'll need for a few more days."

"You're going to stay here then?" She nodded and asked him again what he'd found so funny. "Look what we've done to this room. It was amazing, don't get me wrong, but we certainly know how to break a room in."

There was water everywhere, even on the counter and the mirror over it. There was a puddle near the door, and both towels were soaking wet. Shampoo bottles and bubble bath were spilling over onto the floor, and the curtain had somehow gotten torn down and now lay in a heap near the trash can. She picked up the sponge as it floated by them and tossed it toward the sink across the room.

"There, I cleaned up." Reid laughed harder, and she had

to smile. There was something infectious about his laughter that had her wanting to have him do it more. When his phone rang, she started to move off his lap, then he pulled her back.

"If it's important then they know how to contact me." She let him hold her until she felt him stiffen. "Jodie, Mrs. Campbell just informed me that a being is in town that is using black magic. She said to ask you if you know an Ethan Randolph."

"No. But if he's the guy that tried to kill me, I'd know his face better than his name. We didn't exactly exchange that when he came after me." Jodie stood up when he did, and when he handed her a towel from the linen closet, she hurriedly dried. She had a feeling he was about to get some company.

"They're coming here now. Mrs. Campbell wants to know if you can look at a few pictures for her. And Phil is coming here to talk to us. Also, she said to tell you that your father has been invited." She didn't have any clothes there and tried to think about what he was saying and what the hell she was supposed to wear. Looking at him, he must have seen something there, and he took her into his arms. "We'll get through this. She said to tell you not to worry overly much. If this is the man, you have something on him that he doesn't have about you. You will know his name."

Fat lot of good that was going to do her if he killed her. Or even Reid or one of his family members. When the doorbell rang a few minutes later, she was still dressing in the pair of lounge pants he'd given her and an old sweatshirt. Both were miles too big, and she'd had to roll up the legs of the pants twice, as well as the sleeves on the shirt several times, but she was dressed and ready to face whatever information she was given. Jodie also figured she had a great deal to tell them.

CHAPTER 9

"I don't think I understand. You're saying that you're a thief?" Reid asked, and looked around the room, then back at Jodie. "And you make money at this."

"As I said four times now, I don't steal things that belong to other people. I steal them back for the governments. I only get paid a check, not profit." Jodie sat down and glared at him as she continued. "I'm an international procurer for several countries, including this one."

CJ cleared her throat before she spoke. Reid fully expected her to jump on this with him. She was his ally in this mess. His mate was a thief.

"Do they know you're a shifter?" Jodie shook her head, then nodded. "Ah, I see. Some do and some don't. Probably a good thing. I would imagine that you can get in and out of places others can't. I would imagine that it pays well."

"Yes it does. And since I have next to nothing in ways of personal things, I don't have a house or even an apartment that I have to maintain. I'm sort of a 'ready when they need me' sort of agent." She smiled at CJ. "I've managed to save a little."

"Wait. Wait a minute here. You think this is great?" Reid

nearly fell over when CJ nodded to his question. He looked to Austin, who was smiling too. "Do you have any idea how dangerous this is for her? A thief isn't exactly someone who hasn't pissed a few people off."

"And they don't know who I am." He stared at her. Jodie had to see that this was wrong on so many levels. First of all, she was a thief for the government, and secondly, she was stealing things that other people had stolen. He tried to think of a reasonable way to tell her she was quitting that life and finding something safer to do when she continued. "You say what I think you're going to and I'll tear you a new ass."

Reid growled at Austin and Phil when they laughed. This was not the way he'd thought this would go. Hell, if he told Austin and CJ he was a thief, they'd beat him within an inch of his life and then some. But with her, they seemed to accept the idea.

"Look. I don't want to piss you off, but—"

"Eighteen months ago another country kidnapped the president's daughter. She was sleeping at a friend's house and the Secret Service was all over the place. But this man came in, killed every one of them, the entire family she was staying with, and took her out of the house in less than thirty minutes." Jodie paced as she continued her story. "Along with fifty million dollars, he wanted the president to pardon his brother, who'd killed fifty-three women over the period of nineteen years, and Air Force One."

"I didn't read about that in the paper." She snorted at him and continued on as if he'd not spoken.

"No one was notified because they didn't want anyone to know just how easily he'd done it. And it was easy. He came to the house with pizza's that were drugged. By the time the family was out, he'd managed to kill nine SS men and get back into the house to kill the other four. He shot the family where they were. Once to the head and then the heart. This would include the infant daughter that had only been a month old at the time." CJ asked her when she was called in, but Jodie only had eyes for him. "Four days after the killings, I was notified that my services were needed again. They had the man's name as well as several aliases. I found them twenty-eight hours later."

She didn't continue, and as much as he was sure he didn't want to know how it ended, he needed to know. Without standing, he reached for her hand, and she pulled away. He knew he deserved it but was still hurt by it.

"Were you hurt?" She nodded. "How badly? And where?"

"He'd buried her alive, and I had to dig her out first or she'd be dead. There was a tunnel under his home that he'd dug out and had made a shelter there for her. It was a room about four foot by four foot, and no taller than about six feet. He'd given her a bucket to use, as well as five gallons of water and bags of chips to eat. Nothing else but that. There was no ventilation for her, and when he shut the door to the outside, he'd cut off her air supply. I'm not sure he knew that, but there was no way for me to ask him when I found her." She lifted her shirt and showed him a long pinkish wound that was about eight inches long. "You've seen this yet never asked. But I'll tell you. He cut into me from behind. Brought the knife to my front when I was moving into the house. I was a cat at the time, a large panther. But he knew somehow.

Or he was simply nuts."

Reid stood up and lifted the shirt higher. There was another scar there. Almost the same pink, and he knew she'd gotten it at the same time. He started to ask her about it when she started talking again.

"Delilah was nearly dead when I found her. Had I tried to heal myself, there wouldn't have been enough of me left to heal her. It was her or me, and since I've very little use for myself, she was my top concern." She pulled the shirt back down and took a step back from him. "You think I do this because I'm stealing things. The only time they call me in is when it's a person. I'm fucking good at my job, and I'm not going to stop doing it because you've got some burr up your ass about protecting me. You can't. The sooner you figure that out the better it's going to be for all of you."

"Does she know?" Reid and Jodie both looked at Mrs. Campbell when she asked. "The little girl, does she know who saved her?"

"No. Why would she care?" Reid looked at Jodie when she said that. Before he could tell her that she'd saved her life, that of course she'd want to know, Jodie explained, "I erase their memories anyway. Not of the incident, but of me. It's what's kept me safe all this time. Other than a few people in a few offices across the world, you people are the only ones that know what I do. And if you fuck me over, I'll take you back to the hole I found her in and put you there."

There wasn't any implied threat there but a promise. Reid felt his skin dance as the hair stood up. Even his wolf curled back. She was as scary as she was beautiful, and he had no doubt whatsoever that she'd do just what she said she would.

"His name is Ethan Randolph, and he's a mage, as you know." Mrs. Campbell stood up before anyone could make any more comments on what Jodie had just told them. She handed each of them a thick file. "He's been around for about four hundred years, but it wasn't until the last hundred or so that he's dabbled in the black. Before he was a professor of white magic at the council as well as a consultant at a few murders that involved magic. He was our go to guy."

Reid opened his file but closed it again to move to the other sofa that Jodie had sat on. She wasn't happy that he'd come to her, but right now he needed to be near her. He'd fucked up royally and he wanted more than anything to make it up to her. And he thought the first thing he had to do was trust that she was correct. She was fucking good at her job.

"Those are known murders that we have associated with him. As you can see by the dossier with each person they had quite a bit of magic when they were killed. Two of them were professors with Ethan when he disappeared." Jodie handed him a picture, and he stared at it when Mrs. Campbell came to stand in front of them. "Is that you?"

"It is." Reid couldn't take his eyes off the picture. Jodie continued speaking to Mrs. Campbell, and he looked at what Randolph had done to her. He had no idea how she'd survived, much less was able to get around. He'd torn her apart.

The picture was thankfully in black and white. But Reid had seen enough damage done to bodies while doing his residency that he knew that the dark spill around her was blood. A great deal of it too. And her skin looked as if she'd been peeled open, muscle exposed and even in some places bone. When he flipped the photo over to see what hospital had taken this, he didn't see anything and looked up when someone touched his mind.

"I found her like that. The picture was sent to Hope by me so that they could see what someone had done to her. I had no idea at the time who had harmed her, but I think she did. She may have even known his name too." Tristan nodded to him. When he continued, Reid had a feeling the man was hurting terribly because he'd known she was his daughter. *"She hurt him too. He'll still be hurting from what she'd done to him, I would imagine. Her magic even then was powerful. Now? Well now there is no one as strong as she is."*

"Why?" Tristan asked him what he meant. *"Why is she so strong? Why did he want to kill her for it? Wouldn't he have wanted to learn from her?"*

"In order to absorb her magic, he'd have to kill her with his. It's the way of black magic. And if she dies, all that she is, all her power will go to him. Or when she kills him, which is what I'm hoping, she'll get his. And because of her being so pure, his magic will turn white, and she will be by and far the most powerful being ever created." Tristan paused for several seconds. *"As for why she is so strong? Who knows? It's just the way of the universe."*

Not a great answer, but one he could think on. He'd read enough books to know some about black versus white magic. There was a fine line between the two at the beginning, and many users used both from time to time. That was until they started killing for more. Reid was startled out of his musing

102

when Jodie punched him in the side.

"Are you even here?" He nodded, then smiled. "You're a dork. Pay attention. They're talking about tomorrow. And what they want me to do."

~~~

Tristan wasn't thrilled with the plan. He knew that there were too many variables, and even if Roberson showed up, there was always the off chance that he might simply kill them all. He looked at his daughter as she spoke about some of her abilities. She wouldn't tell them everything, he'd taught her that, but she would give them enough that they'd be able to work with her. Tristan looked at Reid.

He wondered if the young man knew that he was as powerful as his mate. He didn't think either of them had a clue, and was excited to see them together in action. Roberson wouldn't know what hit him when the young wolf tore into him. And Tristan had no doubt that he would eventually have to. For all her power, she was still just as veritable as anyone was. And if Roberson had gotten any stronger, he might be able to hurt her. But Tristan doubted the man could kill her. He'd seen to that.

"Do you think they'll be able to bring him down?" Tristan looked at the lovely alpha bitch sitting next to him. Christ, she was strong too, but he doubted that she'd want to know that either. All of them had something more than they ever used, and he would bet that the lawyer vampire knew it as well.

"I do believe they will. Jolene is very strong, as you know, but she has more now that she and young Reid have mated and bonded. I've taken the liberty of making sure that

103

they both have what I can give them. So, I'm thinking they'll do it." She nodded, then cocked her head. Smiling, he told her the rest. "Yes, in answer to your unspoken question, I've taken both their blood. I would think it better if Phil took it as well, but it is not necessary."

"She's going to leave him if he doesn't get over himself by thinking she needs his protection. She'll work twice as hard to keep him safe than she will herself." Tristan thought the same thing, but CJ continued before he could comment. "Of course, with our family supporting them as well as you, I'm thinking they'll work this out or we'll tie them up until they do."

"She has a home." CJ looked at him when he spoke to her softly. "Several, as a matter of fact. I've made sure that she has everything including her mother's things. I had them put away for her."

"She doesn't know that you plan to meet the sun after she's safe, does she?" He looked at her sharply. "I'm not nearly as stupid as you think I am. And even if you didn't think I was, treating her this way is going to come back and bite you in the ass. She'll not let you go so easily."

"No, I've no doubt that she wouldn't." He looked at Reid and Jolene. "She's so much like her mother. Not just in looks, though she is the exact image of her, but her temperament as well." He laughed when she glared at Reid. "Yes, just like her in her temperament. I think she'll keep the young doctor on his toes."

"He loves her." Tristan nodded at CJ. "I think she loves him as well, but it's harder to tell with her. She keeps her emotions very close to her chest, doesn't she?"

104

"It's what's kept her alive all these years." He glanced at CJ, wanting to tell her the lengths he'd gone to in order to keep Jolene safe and told her. "I've never left her side. Whenever she's gone on a mission, I've been there. It's been difficult at times to let her do her job, but she's never needed me since she learned how to control herself. And so you know, the story about the little girl was much nicer than what really transpired. The little girl wasn't just dying but had died. She'd been dead for several hours before Jolene found her."

"She brought her back?" Tristan nodded. "It's why she's so scared, isn't it? The reason her wounds are still healing. It took a great deal out of her."

"More than you'll ever know."

The plan was set. Jolene would go to the services as planned, but she'd have all of them with her. They had it in their heads that if they went as a group and circled around her, so to speak, she'd be safer. Tristan had his own plan. One that would keep all of them as safe as he could make them.

"I need to speak to you please." Tristan nodded at Hope when she sat beside him. He made sure that he didn't touch her in any way. Her mate was sitting across the room, and while he was part human, he could still do some serious damage to him if Tristan were to touch his mate.

"I'm at your service, as I've always been." Hope snorted at him. "You don't believe me? I think that for as long as we've known each other you should know by now that I do not lie."

"No, but you can bend the hell out of it when it suits

your needs." He smiled but didn't say anything. When she was right, she was right. "Her mother, Jolene's, did Roberson kill her too?"

"He did. He wanted her magic, I think. He had a grudge against me, I believe, as we did have a falling out at one point. And I think that when he ran across her that day, he had no idea who she was. He might not even now. But he does know who Jolene is and her relationship with my mate." He told her that he'd been beneath the ground healing when she'd died. "I never felt her death. I should have, but I was injured so badly that my sleep was powerful. Roberson is the reason I wasn't there to protect her either. I didn't even know Jolene existed until I rose from the earth."

"She's been through a lot with that family. I only know some of it, but CJ knew the older Turner well. She said that he was a great deal like her own father, and he I did know. Austin too. Webber was not a good man. Hell, he wasn't anything but evil. CJ is a wonderful person, and so is your daughter." Hope looked at Reid, then back at him as she continued. "I've watched that boy grow up. When he first came to this family, he was little more than a hood with a chip on his shoulder. Austin straightened him right out and gave him a good and much needed firm hand. Randy too, Reid's younger brother. CJ plucked them right out of the streets they were living on and gave them more than they'd ever had before."

"He is a good man. I can see that. And he's struggling so hard with trying not to be a wolf with her." Tristan laughed. "I wonder, do you know if either of them know what they have?"

"I don't think so. But they're practically brimming over with it." She leaned back in her chair. "The book you gave me through your daughter. Did you know that she never looked in it? Didn't even glance at any of the pages. She would have found out a great deal about her sire and mother if she had."

Tristan nodded. "She's never been one to snoop. If she wants the information, you've my permission to give it to her." Tristan looked at his lady queen from so long ago. "All of it, and nothing varnished over either."

"I will. But in return I would like something from you." He told her anything before thinking and knew he'd regret it. "You'll hang around until they have four children of their own."

"That's an easy one to do, my lady." He kissed the back of her hand and stood up, thinking he'd finally after all these years gotten the best of the queen. "You should know that she cannot have a child. Her body was damaged badly by Roberson when he tried to kill her."

Hope stood up as well and nodded at the couple. "You should know that I have a great many more powers than I did when I was younger, and she is now able to breed as many children as she wants. Don't ever try to fool an old fool, Tristan. I may not be as old as you, but I'm a hell of a lot sneakier."

CHAPTER 10

Ethan felt the magic near him before the knock came at the door. Whoever it was didn't have a great deal of it and more than likely didn't even know that they had it, but he did. When he looked in the peephole, he saw a maid standing there with a set of headphones attached to her ears as well as some wire that ran down her apron to her pocket. His first thought was that kids couldn't go five seconds without some sort of noise, and then he realized she wasn't a kid.

Opening the door, she smiled at him and nodded. "Good morning, sir. I've come to clean the room. Or would you like for me to return later?"

He moved back out of her way and watched as she moved her large cleaning cart into the room. Ethan knew that she was a wolf, but nothing he couldn't handle. So when she went to the bathroom, he finished his coffee and dressed. Ten minutes later, she came out and went to his bed and stripped it clean.

"I'm leaving. I want you to leave an extra coffee packet when you leave, as well as several towels. A set of sheets as well. I may need them later." She nodded, and Ethan smiled. She really didn't have any choice in the matter, as he'd put enough compulsion in his command that there was no way she'd be able to resist. As soon as he moved out of the hotel room and down the hall, his smile broadened. This morning he was going to a funeral and hopefully come back with the girl. The limo pulled up in front of the hotel just as he stepped out.

After giving the man the name of the cemetery, he realized that he was running ahead of schedule. According to the driver, it would take them less than forty minutes to get there, and he had almost an hour and a half.

The driver suggested that he go to the funeral home if he wanted. They would be coming from there and arriving at the graveside soon after. Ethan decided that he'd go to the cemetery and wait. That way he'd be able to hide from the girl and surprise her when it was safe enough to get her.

According to the obituary, there was hardly any family left for the man. He had two sons, and it mentioned them both by name, and a daughter, which it did not. He was curious about that. Why not say her name too unless it was a mistake on the newspapers part? A town this backwards would more than likely make many mistakes in the newspaper and the townspeople would simply not notice it, as they were as hick-town as the editors. Ethan wanted to go back home as soon as possible. He'd felt dirty since he'd walked off the plane.

By the time they arrived at the cemetery, he was excited. He was finally going to kill the girl and absorb all that she was. Actually, that wasn't the only reason he was excited. He was also excited about seeing what her powers merged with his could give him. The girl didn't stand a chance with him.

110

Finding a nice place about a hundred yards from where he'd been told the services were going to be held, he was surprised to see several people milling about. Most of them had some magic surrounding them, but he knew that they weren't who he was looking for. The younger men, he assumed, were the brothers and found that one was a half-wolf, the other human. Not all that smart either if the way they were dressed was any indication.

The taller and by far the heavier of the two was dressed in a pair of sweatpants. The shirt he had on was several sizes too small for him and buttoned crookedly. It was all Ethan could do not to go over to the man and slap him around for not having the intelligence to dress properly.

The other man was little better. While he did have on a pair of pants, they, too, were ill fitting. The hem hit him about two inches above his ankle, and he had on white socks. His shoes, from what Ethan could tell, were sandals and not in very good shape at all. The shirt looked like he'd slept in it, and his hair was just short of being dreadlocks. The pair of them were about as nasty as he'd ever seen.

There were three other men there. Two of them were in very expensive suits and ties, while the third man was sporting a clergyman's collar. He held himself as far away from the first pair as was possible and still be in the same area. The well-dressed men stood off to the side and talked quietly. A few minutes later, a long limo pulled to a stop near them, and then another one right behind it. Ethan stood up and watched as it was emptied of its passengers.

The woman who got out first was beautiful. Long dark hair, and she held the hand of a young man when he alighted behind her. Then three more women came from the car along with two more men. Christ, these were well-moneyed people, Ethan would bet his last nickel on it.

Several more people pulled up in cars and SUVs. By the time someone went to the second limo, Ethan had surmised that he had been wrong about the dead man. He had friends in very high places.

When the girl stepped out of the second limo, he nearly went to her. She had grown to be very lovely. And the way she was dressed also said that she, too, had more than the two scruffy men.

The dark dress she had on fit her body like it had been painted on her. Her hair was down in a loose braid that hung nearly to her hips. Incredibly long legs looked like she worked out more than she ever sat, and when the man who slipped out of the limo behind her put his arm around her waist, she leaned against him. Ethan's only thought was this was better than he'd ever thought.

He'd gotten more magic by buying off a boyfriend or girlfriend than he'd ever thought was possible. Over the years he'd simply gone to the other partner, promised them a great deal of money, and then killed them later when he'd gotten what he wanted. Shit, he'd had the best of both worlds as far as he was concerned.

The ill-dressed men walked toward her. When the man with her stepped in front of her, Ethan had to laugh. If she was even half of what she was back then, she didn't need his help. But when the heavier of the two men drew back his hand to hit her, one of the first men stepped up behind him and grabbed his arm. He was on the ground before Ethan could take a breath.

"She's lovely, isn't she?" Ethan turned slowly to look at the old man standing next to him. Ethan looked around, wondering how he'd managed to sneak up on him like that. When he saw a car a few yards away, he looked back at the man.

"All women are lovely until they open their mouths. Unless it's to do something productive with it like suck me off." He was crude and he knew it, but instead of pissing the man off, he laughed.

"I'm sure the young buck with her would tear you apart if he heard you talking about her like that. And from all accounts, she's a nice girl too." The old man seemed to be a little less friendly than he'd been before. Ethan started to tell him to fuck off when the old man continued, "Then again, I might do it myself."

Ethan felt his skin crawl. It was one thing to say those things, but to have someone standing this close threaten him made him take a step back. He started to tell the old man to go away when he had a deeper fear of the man. Ethan took another step back. Before he could figure out what he was feeling, someone screamed behind them.

Turning, Ethan was surprised to see the heavier man lying on the ground and the woman standing over him. He couldn't hear what was being said, but he was pretty sure that the man was begging for her to back off. Ethan took a step toward them when the man beside him grabbed his arm.

"I wouldn't if I were you. Her magic will kill you, and I'm just not ready for you to kick the bucket right now." The man faded out, and his laughter lingered long after Ethan turned back to the people at the graveside. Before he could think about what he was doing, he ducked behind the tree he was next to and stood there waiting.

He knew the voice of the older man. Ethan wasn't sure how he knew him, but he did. Somewhere in his long past, he and the other man had crossed paths, and Ethan had a feeling he was coming back for more. Moving toward the street in the opposite direction of the funeral, he made his way to the street. Hailing a cab was not his first choice, but the limo was long gone and he wasn't walking all the way back to the hotel.

Even after he arrived at his room, he was still shaking, and the harder he tried to remember the man, the more elusive he became. Finally, he sat down after pacing what seemed to be miles and miles of walking to nowhere. Ethan closed his eyes and let his mind wander over the man's features.

Grey hair didn't really help him. Ethan rarely associated with anyone that had it, and since he'd been using black magic, his own hair had turned white. Gray-blue eyes didn't help either. Ethan wasn't sure if they were actually gray-blue or if the light was playing tricks on him. The sun had shown them as blue, but when he'd been in the shade for a few seconds, they'd looked dark gray.

The man was perhaps in his seventies. Maybe even his eighties. He wasn't tall, maybe about five foot five or a little shorter. There was nothing about him that rang a bell, and even less about him that made him memorable to anyone, including him. Ethan was now afraid. Very afraid.

~~~

Austin wanted to laugh. Jodie could see that from across

114

the room. His face was tight with it, and the way he kept putting his fist into his mouth made her think that when he did let loose he was going to be in a great deal of pain. CJ glared at him before turning to her.

"Jodie, what did your brother mean that you'd stolen his home from him? Surely he doesn't think you should have turned the land and house over to him after you'd caught up with all the taxes and made sure the house was kept up." Jodie watched as Reid and his brother walked in before she answered CJ.

"He does, and so does Mike. They don't think that as a woman I should have the brains to have a job, much less the means to pay bills." She pulled away from Reid when he sat nearly atop her. "They are both lazy bastards and will now have to find other means of…. Will you please stop touching me?"

Jodie flushed when Austin burst out laughing. The poor man was going to pay for that if his mate's look at him was any indication. But Reid was the touchiest man she'd ever met.

"No, I don't think so." Reid had said that like he'd taken great care in considering her request. She was going to knock him on his ass as soon as she could. "You have the most amazing skin, did you know that?"

She growled. He was making her so needy with the way he was constantly touching her, breathing on her and simply being around her. She tried once again, knowing it would be futile, to move away, only this time he picked her up and put her on his lap. When she shifted, he held her still, and she felt his thickening cock.

"Behave or the rest of the room will see just where I want to touch you." His voice whispered through her mind, and she looked at him. *"I want you. I need to mark you again after your brother touched you. And I will, but if you don't let me have this now, we're going to go upstairs right now and I'm going to say to hell with this meeting."*

She watched the others talk, thinking about what had happened at the cemetery. Mike had been so pissed that the police had shown up this morning and told him they had twenty-four hours to get out or they'd be physically removed that he'd hit her in the mouth as soon as she stood near the grave. Curt was just as pissed, but he'd tried to kill her by going for her throat. Reid had moved so fast that he'd even startled her.

Curt was lifted off the ground and held there for several seconds before she was able to get Reid to release him. And even then he'd tossed him to the ground, where he'd hit his head on the headstone next to them. She'd thought him dead, but when he sat up and glared at her, she knew she couldn't be so lucky. She thought that Austin was going to get hurt as well when he pulled her back out of the way and Mike had stupidly attacked him. The man had no brains was all she could think of. But she'd been so afraid for them all, she'd used some of her magic.

"Jodie?" She looked at Nancy, as she had insisted she call her. "Are you all right, dear? You look done in."

"I'm fine." Nancy wiggled her finger for her to follow her, and she got up after telling Reid where she was going. The kitchen, Jodie had discovered, was Nancy's domain. "Really, I'm fine. I just get a little…stressed, I guess, when I

116

talk to Mike and Curt."

"What do you think you're doing?" Jodie took a step back when she saw the spoon in the woman's hand. She'd heard about that thing, and she wasn't going to be a victim of it if she could help it. "Are you trying your best to make me upset?"

"No, ma'am." Nancy told her to sit down, and she did. She didn't think she'd used anything more than her "mom" voice, but Jodie was a little afraid. "I'm not trying to upset anyone. Well, except for Reid. But he's the one that is driving me over the edge."

Nancy sat down after giving her a large glass of juice. "Drink that. And while you do, I'm going to tell you something."

"I'm not going to be able to leave here, am I?" Nancy shook her head. "It would be better for him if I did. I'm not what you'd call a nice person, and I'm certainly not a doctor's mate material."

"Why not?" Jodie looked at Nancy. "What do you think a doctor's wife is like? A woman who could give tea parties? Sit for long periods of time listening to other women prattle on and on about nothing." She huffed. "I think that a doctor's wife should be just what you are. Someone who makes her mate happy as well as protects him when he's too tired or just being too manly to do so himself. You can do all those things."

"He can take care of himself better if I don't bring my crap down on him. Like today for instance. Reid would never have been in that predicament had I not been a part of his life." Jodie squirmed on the chair when Nancy picked up the spoon. "Are you planning to hit me with that?"

"Are you going to make me?" They stared at each other for several minutes. Jodie had a feeling she was being sized up, and for some reason she didn't want the older woman to find her lacking. When she put the spoon back down, Jodie let out a breath she didn't know she was holding.

"I'm a thief." Nancy shook her head. "What would you call what I do? I'm not very nice when I go and get back what I need. I've killed plenty and will more than likely kill a great many more."

"And you'll come home at night because of it. Do you really think of yourself as a thief or someone who helps others? That child you told us about? Do you suppose she would think of you as a thief if she could remember you? I doubt it very much. Nor do her parents."

"I do steal things when I'm in the house." Jodie wanted her to see what she was and not coat it in honey. "I found some artifacts once that I knew belonged to another country, one I wasn't working for. I didn't tell that guy what I'd done. I just—"

"And what did you do with the artifacts? Do you have them in a vault somewhere? Do you have them stashed in one of those rental units with all the other things you've taken?" She snorted at her again. "No, if I know you well enough I'd say you returned it to the country it belonged to and didn't even take credit for it."

Jodie got up to pace. This woman was too smart for her own good. Every time she thought she had a reason for her to turn her out, she'd have an equally good reason for her to stay. Jodie turned to look at her.

118

"I can't have children. Ever." Nancy nodded but said nothing. "Reid knows, but he said he doesn't care. He even knew before I told him."

"He's a good doctor. I'm sure he would have figured it out. And what did he say when you tried to tell him?" Jodie flushed. "Just as I thought. He didn't care, did he?"

"No. He said that there were lots of children out there that needed parents for one reason or another and that—" Jodie sat down. "I don't want to love him. I don't…what if he gets tired of me? Or if he thinks he can do better?"

The spoon was whacking her in the head before she could blink. Man, it fucking hurt too. But she only glared at Nancy when she held it out to strike again.

"You say another thing like that and I'll beat you within an inch of your life." Nancy got up and poured her more juice, her hands shaking as she continued. "He loves you. And you do him. Though I doubt either of you have enough sense to say it to the other. As for him doing better? How do you suppose he's going to do that? When he loves you enough to nearly kill for you?"

"I didn't ask him to do that." Jodie eyed the spoon when Nancy did, but neither of them made a move to grab it. Jodie took a deep breath as she told her what she'd only discovered today. "And I do love him. I don't want to for the simple reason he's going to figure this out and want to toss me over for some women that looks good on his arm. Much better than I do."

"And why would I do that when you look so good there?" Jodie closed her eyes when she heard Reid speak behind her. Nancy got up and moved by her, patting her on the shoulder as she left the room. When Reid sat down across from her, she wanted to crawl into a hole, but he took her hands into his. "I love you as well."

CHAPTER 11

Curt watched the fucking police officer put a large padlock on the door. The hasp alone had to weigh ten pounds, and he'd attached it to the front door with the biggest screwdriver he'd ever seen. The other cop was doing the same to the back door. Curt looked at Mike as he seemed to be fighting tears. Fucking moron.

He'd had a pounding headache after being thrown around by that bastard yesterday. He looked down at the blood on his shirt and wanted to find the guy right now and kill him. But he was slightly afraid of him…well, honestly he was terrified of the big wolf. And the alpha made him want to wet his pants he'd been so afraid of him. Curt was going to make them all pay.

"You'll move off this property now and never return. The new owners will be making improvements as soon as tomorrow. I would—"

Curt cut him off. "She can't sell this land. It belongs to me." Curt glanced at his brother. "Me and my brother. We been taking care of our dad for months now and he didn't say a word about nobody else buying it."

"Be that as it may, but it's been legally sold to Mr. Force.

And he is telling us that if you set foot on this property again he'll have you prosecuted to the fullest extent of the law. Do you understand?" Curt wanted to tell him that he understood all right. He understood that Jodie was going to fucking pay for this, and so was that Mr. Force.

"Where might I find Mr. Force?" He knew where the man lived. It was something he'd known from the moment he'd stepped into his territory all those months ago. "I'd like to have a few words with him."

"You do that. And you know as well as I do where he is." The man let a little of his wolf go and had Curt taking a step back. "You fuck with my alpha, and I'll come hunting you down and tear you into so many pieces that they'll never find you even with dogs."

Curt and Mike were escorted to the edge of the property, and the officer that had threatened him stood watching for several minutes as he and Mike started walking. Each of them had a large trash bag of their clothes and a blanket and pillow. That was all they were allowed to take. Anything else was deemed part of the property by their sister, and she was the one that had made a list of things that belonged to them. How the hell she'd known what they had was beyond him, but it was exact right, down to the five socks that he'd had when he arrived.

"She gave us a hundred dollars." Curt looked at Mike when he was holding the envelope in his hand that the officer had given him. "I guess she didn't have to do that, the cop told me he wouldn't have. But what are we supposed to do with only this much? Hotels like we should be staying in cost way more than this."

"Twice that I would guess. And then what are we supposed to do for food or even a way to get around? You know she got way more than this for our land. She should have at least given me seventy percent of what she got. Beings how I'm the oldest." Mike stared at him as if he might disagree. "You think you should have gotten as much as me? Christ, Mike, I've been putting up with dad way longer than you have and her shit too. Not to mention me being a wolf. I got more needs than you being only a stupid human."

"You're only half wolf, and I'm pretty sure that I have just as many needs as you. Food and a place to sleep are needed by us both, and other than something to get around in, that's all you need too." Mike put his money in his pocket and smiled. "And if you blow all of yours on stupid fucking shit, know that I'm not sharing."

Curt saw red. His wolf, never a very stable part of his life, seemed to surge forward in what felt like a heartbeat. He was tearing at his brother's throat in seconds and killed him in less than that. His wolf was still drinking from his wound when he heard a car coming and took off to the woods so no one would see him. Curt heard the first shot fired just as he cleared the tree line.

He'd killed him. And not only that, because of the fact that someone had seen him, he'd not been able to get his money either. Curt was shifting to his human when he realized that he'd lost his own as well.

"Mother fucking son of a fucking bastard bitch." He grabbed his head as he continued. "That fucking stupid crotch waffle goblin is going to pay for this. This is Jodie's fault, and that dicknosed cock knob alpha's too. I'm fucking his son, and I deserve to have what she does."

Curt paced the woods naked until he cut his foot open on a rock. Dropping to the ground, he pulled out the dirt and other things and sat there crying. He was glad he was alone because if anyone saw him right now he'd have to kill them too.

"Showed you to fuck with your older brother, didn't I? You elastic taint biscuit fuck-tard." Curt was having fun now even with the tears. "Pie-eating douche crotch jockey. I should knock you on your pompous sphincter smelly shart boner."

He sat here laughing hard enough to hurt as he strung together word after word, not even caring if they made sense any longer. By the time he had put together slutty turd pirate hammer sphincter, he was lying down and laughing. It was the first good laugh he'd had in a while. Sitting up, he looked around the cold forest.

"Now what?" Curt had no money, no clothes, and he wasn't in any position to get either of them in the near future. His brother was dead, and his sister, who he hated, was living in the lap of luxury with a full-blooded wolf. Curt wondered where things had gone so wrong for him. He got up to find some shelter and gathered wood at the same time.

"I've been a good man. Well, not good I guess, but I've done some nice things." Curt tried to think what things he might have done and came up with nothing. For some reason that pissed him off too. As he was stomping through the woods, he started talking to himself again because he was suddenly depressed about what everyone had done to him.

"Jodie did this to us. She had to have her way and move

off." He tried to remember why she'd moved and smiled. "Of course, I could have hit her a little less or maybe not have stolen from her so much either, but she was always having things that I wanted. Like them books. What the hell did she need all them books for? It's not like she was going to go to college or nothing."

But she had, he thought. And had done well at it too, he'd bet. She had that nice bike too. Why would anyone give a loan to a girl who was as stupid as she was anyway? When Curt found a cave about an hour from where he'd been, he crawled into it and tried to start a fire.

He finally gave up an hour later when he was too cold and damp to fuck with it anymore. When he curled into a tight ball and tried to sleep, he thought about his sister again and how she was probably wearing silk and sleeping in a big bed. He was going to make her pay if it was the last thing he did.

~~~

The human had died almost instantly, they'd said. Ethan looked at the mauled body of the man from the cemetery and knew that it was a wolf that had killed him, and he was pretty sure that a couple of the cops knew it too. He heard one of them call someone and tell them what he'd found.

"He's been murdered by another wolf. Yeah, I think so. His scent is all over the place." He paused for a long time and Ethan wished he could have heard the other end of the conversation when the cop laughed. "Yeah, he left his money as well as his brothers behind when he shifted. I wonder how far he got when he realized what he'd done."

After much debate on where the wolf was now, naked

and broke, the cop hung up. When he stilled, Ethan had a feeling he knew he was nearby, but Ethan knew that his magic was hiding him from everyone. The man was just being cautious. When the cop told the coroner to load the body up, Ethan tried to think of where he would go if he was a wolf, and decided to see if he could find Curt in the woods. It had been easier than he'd thought. Ethan found the man about two hours after the police left the scene.

He couldn't track the wolf by his scent, but he could follow foot prints. The man had walked in circles for a long time after he'd shifted, so that Ethan wondered if he'd been lost. When he'd found his tracks again, he was surprised that the dumb animal had survived this long after he'd seen where he was sleeping. The man was in a den with five bears not fifteen feet from where he rested.

"Get up." The man moaned but didn't wake. Ethan kicked him in the head. "I said to get up. I have something for you."

He looked like he might shift and Ethan held him. There was no way he had time to fuck with a pissed off wolf, and would just as soon kill him if he tried anything. Ethan tossed a pair of pants and a shirt at him. When the man picked them up, he threw shoes at him as well.

"Who the fuck are you?" Ethan shook his head. No way would he give this man his name even if there was a chance that he'd know what he'd given him. Instead, he asked him what his name was. "Curtis Andrew Turner the fifth. My dad was Curtis, so they called me Curt."

Too much information, but just what Ethan wanted. A full name and a sire's name as well. *This was much too easy,*

126

he thought. Turning his back to the fat man, he told him to get dressed.

"I want the name of the woman that hit you at the cemetery." The man denied her hitting him and that he'd fallen. "Whatever. I want her name and what she is to you."

"My sister. And her name is Jodie Turner. She's a fucking bitch." Ethan savored the name of the woman while the man continued to berate her. "You should have seen her when she was younger. Nothing but a pain in the ass then and now, but she knew who was boss."

"I just bet she did." When the man stood up, Ethan turned to look at him. "Have you no pride in yourself? Do you realize that your shirt is done up incorrectly and your shoes are untied?" He nearly told him to fix it when he realized that changing the man's appearance by touching him would alert the other shifters.

"You're going to be staying with me, and as such, you'll learn to dress properly. Button your shirt and tuck it in." Curt glared at him, and Ethan tossed him against the cave wall twice before he let him drop to the ground. "The bears will have a tasty treat of you if you'll not listen to me."

Curt looked back into the darkness of the cave and stepped out into the sunshine. Like it would do him any good. If the bears were to wake from the sleep he'd put them in when he'd arrived, they'd be able to outrun the man before he had a chance to get his shoes tied properly. When he was finished making the best of himself, Ethan willed them both to his hotel room. He'd long since decided that the man was going to die, but first he wanted as much information from him as he could get, starting with what he knew about the

127

family that Jodie was staying with. Ordering up some lunch for them both, then doubling it for the man as his last meal, Ethan sat downwind from the nasty smelling man and settled in to question him.

"Is her name short for anything other than Jodie?" Curt looked confused. "Your sister, is Jodie short for anything, or was she christened Jodie?"

"She ain't never been to no church as far as I know. My dad hated religion, and she weren't no better when she lived at home. But her name has always been Jodie so far as I know. Dad never called her anything but that when he had a mind to call her anything." Ethan was going to have a major headache, he just knew it. "Course she wasn't really my sister, but I don't think she knows that."

"What?" Ethan must have startled the man, because he backed off. Taking several deep breaths, he tried to calm himself before he asked him again. "What do you mean she's not your sister? How do you know this?"

"When we were little, I asked my dad why she could shift and not me or Mike." He looked out the window when he said his brother's name. "She's going to pay for him dying like he did. There was no reason for her to come between us. Her being a kid my momma took in when I was little."

"You're saying she's not anything to you? Not even a half or step-sister?" Curt shook his head. "Then why did you say she was your sister? Why didn't you simply tell me when I asked you what she was to you?"

"Didn't think about it until just now. She's always just been Jodie Turner, my pain in the ass sister. Anyways, Dad said she was raised up by Mom before he got out of jail, so he

128

didn't have the heart to tell her she couldn't keep her. Then when Mom died, she was useful around the house until she got it in her head she was leaving us. There wasn't nobody to clean up after us anymore either. That's when I lighted out. But I comed back when Dad called me."

Her name wasn't Turner. And for some reason he doubted that her first name was Jodie either. Ethan went to the door to let the man in with the food and let him set it up while he tried to think what to do. Ethan was finding less and less use for Curt all the time.

Curt was eating his third plate of food when Ethan was finishing his salad. The man not only looked like a pig but he ate like one too. There was food on his shirt as well as hanging from his chin. And Ethan wasn't sure, but he thought there was ham in his hair. Before he could tell him to wash up, hc belched so loudly that Ethan was sure the neighbors heard him.

"That was right fine." Ethan couldn't eat anything else with this man sitting across from him, and wasn't surprised when he said he'd take what he'd not eaten. Before he killed the man outright, he got up and went to the bedroom for a few seconds to regain control. His temper wasn't the best when he was stressed out, and he was afraid of killing the man in the hotel room, and people knowing it was him. The phone ringing startled him.

"People are going to think you had something to do with his brother's death if you keep him around you." Ethan knew the voice. It was the man from the cemetery. "He murdered his own brother and will more than likely try and kill you if I don't miss my bet."

"Who is this? How did you know he was here?" Ethan looked around the room when he heard the old man laugh. "You're not human, are you?"

"Got it in one." The man laughed again. "You're not nearly as stupid as I first thought you were. But have you figured out who I am yet? Have you a clue who I might be from your past?"

The line went dead, and Ethan held the receiver in his hand like he was expecting someone to take it from him. The man knew that Curt was there. That frightened him more than he could think, because if he knew and the stupid man turned up dead, he'd know he'd done it. Ethan put the receiver down and went to the living room where Curt was laying back on the couch and sleeping. The moron had covered himself with the otherwise unused napkin like it was a blankie. Ethan sat down to think.

She wasn't Jodie Turner, and she wasn't related to this man. So killing him would only link him to the murder as well as his brother's death. The man on the phone knew him from sometime in the past, and Ethan had a feeling it wasn't something that was nice. He glared at the fucking bastard across from him. This was not turning out to be nearly as easy as he'd hoped.

The wolf that had been holding her was his only hope. If he could get the man to see reason and give her up, he'd be home free and whatever powers that she had would be his. He'd no doubt that she'd never even realized she had them and she did have a great many. She was going to be his, and soon too. He needed what she had desperately. Ethan decided to let the man sleep while he tried to think who the caller was. He closed his eyes, and instead of thinking about his looks, concentrated instead on his voice.

In all his years, he'd met up with millions of beings like the old man. But he didn't think the man was human, and now that he knew the man was someone from his past for sure, he no longer thought he was as old looking as he'd thought. His first thought was vampire and he went with that.

There were nine or ten of them that he'd had dealings with in the recent past. Three he'd killed, so he knew that it couldn't be them, and the other half dozen or so would never have contacted him. But he still thought about their voice. No, none of them. As he was trying to think about other beings, he came back to the vampires. He just knew it was them.

One in particular kept at him. This man, a very old and very strong vampire, had been chasing him for some reason. Not that it mattered, but Ethan thought of the dead man anyway. There was something so…Ethan opened his eyes, staring at nothing while the incident with the man played out.

"You'll not get it," the man had said to him as he held the book tightly to his chest. "It's not for a man like you."

Ethan tried to concentrate on the book to think what it had been when it occurred to him. It was the book of vampires, the beginning. Ethan thought it was called the *Book of Life*. The first book that they'd brought when vampires first came here.

"I'll have it and kill you for thwarting my plans." Ethan had moved forward toward the vamp only to come up against a wall. The vamp had been stronger than he'd thought, and for a small second that had made him nervous. And when he was nervous, Ethan used his magic as if he had so much to spare, when in reality back then, he'd had very little. He was pulling from the elements, stealing what wasn't his, when the man spoke again.

"You'll regret this." Ethan had laughed at the vampire as he spoke softly. *"Sed ad locum, ubi tu mihi nemo poterit. Dilectus meus mihi, et ego non nisi redibis nomen."*

The book disappeared, and it had taken him several seconds to translate the Latin he'd spoken. *Go to a place where no one will find you but me. You'll return to me only if I say my beloved's name.* He unleashed on the vampire. His temper got the better of him, and he simply let himself go.

"Mother fuck." Ethan stood up and paced, concentrating harder on the voice. It was him, he knew it, but he'd killed him. There was no way for him to have survived the blast that had hit him.

Still he looked down at the man in front of him, not really seeing him but aware of him. Leaning over slowly, he sniffed the man and staggered back. It was the vampire. His scent was on the half breed, but more than that, so was the girl. The girl smelled just like the vamp.

"Shit. Shit, shit, shit." She'd been with the vampire. Whoever they were, whatever they wanted, wasn't going to be good for him. They were conspiring together to harm him, and that just would not do.

CHAPTER 12

They were finally all gone. Reid watched Jodie as she moved around the room touching things, but he'd bet if he asked her she'd not know what they were. He had a feeling that she was trying to work up the courage to say something to him, and she thought it would upset him. Reid was in love, and right now she could tell him she had three heads and he'd not care.

Reid let her think. He had some thinking to do on his own. The things that she'd told him in the kitchen had frightened him a little. He could shift too, into anything that he wanted. So far he'd only thought about it, but doing it was what had him a little nervous. He also had fangs, something he'd been able to feel in his mouth since she'd told him. When she spoke, he looked at her, pushing his fear away.

"When I first got here, I healed a little boy. I didn't get his name, but he'd hit his head pretty hard running after some little girls." She turned from the framed picture she was looking at to stare at him. "When I did that, healed him, I took a little of him into me."

She shifted so suddenly that he felt his breath catch. Before him was standing Connor's little boy, Allen. He was bloodied on his forehead, and when he...she smiled at him, he smiled back. Then Jodie was herself again.

"I'm assuming because you took some of him in you, you can be him." She nodded. "And me as well?"

Again, the shift was seamless and instant. She was him right down to the clothing he had on and the small bruise on his hand where he'd hit Mike earlier. Sitting up, he asked her to shift back. It was very...strange was an understatement, but that's all his befuddled mind could capture as a word right now.

"I can shift into anyone who's touched me as well." Nancy, Hope, Austin, and Dallas moved over her body in fluid motion until he was nearly ill from it. "I can touch anyone and become them, but only the ones I take into me, from healing or...sex...can I talk like them. I can also control their thoughts. Not yours for some reason, but I can be you."

"Don't." He looked up at her. "Please don't shift like that for a little while. I'm still...Christ, I'm not sure, but I think I'm about as overwhelmed as a person can be."

"You can as well." Reid leaned back and stared at her as she moved toward him. "Anyone. You're my mate as much as I am yours. Anything I can do, think, or be, you can as well."

"No, I don't think so. When someone is changed... converted, I guess...there's something that happens. Nothing has happened to me. I'm still the same." She straddled his lap so that she was facing him and nodded. "Okay, then tell me how to do it and I'll show you."

"Think of...anyone you've touched. You're the touchiest man I know. Anyone you're near, you have to put your hands on them." She smiled, and he realized she was trying to calm him. "Think of your alpha, Austin. Close your eyes and think of him."

There wasn't any pain, though why he thought there would be he had no idea. But when he looked at her, he knew that he was no longer Reid Atkins but Austin Force. He lifted his hands and looked at them. It was the one thing that he'd always admired about Austin. He had the biggest hands, but they could be so gentle. Especially when he put them out for you as a lifeline, as he'd done for him and his brother countless times.

"What about animals? Do I have to touch them as well to become them?" His voice, while not his own, didn't seem to bother her. She shook her head and stood up.

"We can go outside, and you can do it. But I need to caution you on a couple of things. There are some problems with shifting to animals you're not familiar with." He asked her what kind. "I use a hawk quite a bit. And it took me a while to get the feathers right so that I wasn't all one color. And flying can be a bitch until you get used to it."

"I can see that." He stood up as well, and when she took a step back from him, he pulled her to his body. "What I'm really hoping is that I can convince you to shift into your wolf and let mine fuck you."

Her response was intense. Jodie moaned and buried her nose in his throat and licked him. Reid held her not because he wanted to touch her…he did…but because he was afraid he'd fall if he didn't.

"You should know that now that you shift, it's no longer necessary for you to be naked." She nipped at his pounding pulse, and he gripped her tighter. "But I'd love to see you naked. I love the play of your muscles when you move, the way your skin ripples over your chest, and your nipples when they get hard."

"Jodie, I'm not going to make it if you keep this up." He pulled her head back by taking a handful of her hair and yanking her back. "I want you."

"I'm yours." Taking her by the hand, he led her to the door that spilled out onto the back deck. It was a private deck from this room, but the rest of the house from the back of the house had access to a bigger one as well. He moved past the hot tub, wondering if it was working when the jets suddenly turned on. Then he nodded in satisfaction. He'd have to thank Tristan for it. There wasn't one there when he'd bought the house.

"Strip." Jodie stared at him for all of two seconds when she started to unbutton her blouse. She was slow, and her fingers fumbled twice. Finally his wolf decided that he'd been patient enough and snarled. Reid tore it from her body. "Christ, I want you now."

The wolf startled him for several seconds when Jodie shifted. She was much bigger than he'd expected, and she was silver, not black like he was. When he called his to him, his own wolf moved along his skin quickly, absorbing his clothes as if he was wearing nothing. He blinked twice and noticed that she'd changed to black.

"I want you to be silver. It's beautiful on you." Starting at her muzzle, she shifted back to the silver, and he moved along her body. *"Do you have any idea how beautiful you are?"*

"I'm a dog, so no, I don't." Reid nipped at her shoulder as he passed her, and she growled low. *"I don't become a wolf much. My brother could find me better when I was."*

"You'll not have to worry about him. I know that you can protect yourself, but so long as he's a threat, I'll do my best to keep you safe." She nodded and looked out into the woods. *"Go. Run so that I can chase you down."*

The leap over the railing was almost as if she'd been on springs. She was running to the woods as his wolf sniffed the air. She was his, and she was aroused. Taking off after her, Reid paused for a second to let the other wolves on the property know that he and his mate were out there and that they wanted to be left alone. Randy laughed at him.

"A man gets one night off to go have some fun and what do you do? You rain on my parade." Randy laughed again as he continued. *"I saw her just now. Christ, she's fucking huge and silver. What the hell? You have a silver wolf? She and CJ are going to be amazing together. One white and one silver."*

He saw his brother leave the woods. Randy and he had talked about the house and his wanting to live alone for a while. He'd also confessed that he wasn't ready to find a mate right now, and if he had a house, then women would be swarming all over him.

"You know they think that because you have a mortgage then you must be stable or something. Broke is all you are, and I'm not…I don't want to settle down. I need to build up my practice, and Phil is going to help me with that. Do you understand?" Reid assured him that he did. "That money Mom and Dad had, do you think you'll use it now?"

"I don't know yet. I have a mate, one that I want to

give everything to, so maybe." Randy nodded, and Reid felt compelled to tell him all of it. "We can't have children. Jodie was hurt some time back and she can't have children of her own. But we might adopt. If we do, I'm not going to be a parent anything like ours were."

"The more…CJ and Austin saved our lives. I don't mean because we almost got Austin to kill us by being stupid, but we would never have survived if they hadn't taken us in. I know that now." Reid nodded, knowing that what his brother said was true. "We owe them everything."

"I don't think they'd see it that way, but you're right." They'd talked a bit more before Randy had left. That was two days ago and things seemed to be back to normal for the two of them now.

Just as he started to search for Jodie, he saw her moving. She was low to the ground, and he wanted to move up behind her and tackle her, then take her to the ground. When she turned back to look at him, Reid felt as if he'd been given a great and amazing gift. He was so much in love with his mate that he ached with it. He moved slowly to her, thinking of all the ways he was going to show her how much he loved her.

~~~

Jodie had felt him behind her. She'd only turned to see how close he was when he started walking to her. Stalking was a better term for how he moved, like sex on two legs. When she stood up, he didn't slow but continued that slow steady walk that told her that she was his.

"*Your brother was here.*" He nodded but didn't say anything. "*He said we were messing up his day off. I didn't*

138

know that he used these woods too."

"There were any number of wolves here as well as a couple of cats. Austin has made it known that others can use the land, and sometimes it spills over into ours. Does it bother you?" She told him it didn't. *"The land that Austin bought from you, he's going to make into a sort of open fields so that anyone can use them. He said we'll maintain it, but it will be a gathering place for all species."*

"That'll be nice." He was standing close enough now that she could touch him and ran her body down his to mark him. *"You smell like him. Your brother. I have his scent now."*

"I want you." She nodded at him and moved to face him. When he circled her, she stood as still as she could until he was behind her. *"Do you know how delicious you smell to my wolf? You're driving him insane with need."*

"Please." Jodie thought her body was going to combust she needed him so badly. When he mounted her from behind, she felt her body respond with a fire that she knew he'd feel once he touched her. His low growl made her think that he could smell her too.

Her wolf fought him. Jodie wasn't really sure why because she wanted him as much as he did her, but fight she did. When he sank his teeth into her shoulder, Jodie cried out not from pain but from the intensity of the emotions that went with it. As soon as he had her shoulders to the ground, he entered her, and she growled.

"Christ, you're so tight." He slammed into her hard, and she growled again. *"Don't move. I swear I'm barely holding him back now."*

"Fucking take me, Reid. I need it." The growl from him

ran along her skin, and she knew that he was still fighting for control. But she shifted beneath him then, and he took her hard. She wanted to come, needed to, but he wasn't giving her what she needed. When he tore at her shoulder, the pain this time took her breath away, but the pain was soon replaced with the most incredible connection she'd ever had with another person. As soon as she felt it, she knew that he was close to coming and moved again. When Reid touched her sweet spot, her body reacted as if he'd pressed a button. She came screaming out his name.

Reid lifted his head from her as her body continued to vibrate with her release. When he roared, the hair on her body danced, making every nerve ending feel like he was sending currents to them. His command to shift had her rolling to her back and bringing her human forward all at once.

"I want to taste you." She nodded as he stood up over her. "Christ, coming in you like that was fucking fantastic, but now I want to drink from you."

His cock strained from his body, and she wanted to touch him. But when she reached for him, he told her no. He was too close. She knew the feeling, so when he dropped to his knees before her, fisting his cock, she sat up on her elbows to look at him.

"You're beautiful like this. Naked and hard. Do you know how much I want to take you into my mouth again and suck you?" He shivered, and she ran her foot over his chest to his cock, curling her toes around him before he rocked into her foot. "Can you come on me like this?"

"Yes, but if I don't taste you now, I'm going to fucking die." Moving his hands up her thighs, he lifted her up off the

140

ground so that only her shoulders were touching. He never took his eyes off her when he licked her from gate to clit. "Delicious. Just as I knew you would be."

He didn't just lick her but devoured her. Every time she thought she was going to come, he would move to some other erogenous place on her body until she was ready to reach between her legs and show him what she needed. Suckling her clit was driving her insane with need, her nether lips were nibbled on until she was dizzy with it. Every time he fucked her with his tongue she felt it to her head, but it was never enough. And begging him didn't do anything but make him tease her more.

"Do you want to come?" She nodded, no longer capable of speech, at least anything that made sense. "If I let you come, will you let me fuck you again? Take you from behind while I play with this pretty pussy of yours."

"Anything. Please anything. I need to come." She screamed when he bit her clit, and when he commanded her to come, she felt as if she were poised on a great mountain and was ready to freefall when suddenly she did just that. She came so hard, for so long that her voice was thick with it, her body like a coiled spring that when she let go the second time and then the third, it was all she could do to hang onto consciousness.

But he wasn't finished with her. Almost as soon as he let her go, she was being flipped to her belly. His hands jerked her hips up almost as soon as she could get her knees under her, and he was deep inside of her before she could take a breath. And then he covered her with his body.

"I love having you this way." He nipped at her earlobe

when he whispered in her ear. "You're mine and now that I have you here, I'm going to never let you go."

"I don't want to leave you." She realized in that moment that she didn't. "I won't leave you. I swear. I love you, Reid."

"And I you." He moved slowly, making her ache again, her need spiking up until she wanted him to let her come again. "You're in heat. I didn't know that before or even with the damage you sustained that you'd do that, but Christ, my wolf knows it and wants to fuck you."

The pain of not being able to give him children ran through her, but he didn't let her dwell on it. When she started to pull away, he growled low and told her not to leave him.

"Your scent is so sweet right now. The smell of your skin is like spring in Washington when the cherries are in bloom." Her body started to respond to his words, and she moved back with each of his forward strokes. "I want you to mark me, Jodie. I want to feel your teeth sink into my flesh and tear at me. Will you mark me?"

She nodded, and he moved off her to roll over. As soon as she was on her back, she lifted her knees to her chest as he filled her again. Reid offered her his throat, and when he did, she licked along the pounding vein until she found his pulse. As soon as he told her, screamed really, that he was coming, she sank her fangs deep into his throat and drank from him. This time when she came, she barely sealed the wounds with her tongue before she let the darkness take her.

She woke once when he laid her on the bed. Curling into him when he laid down beside her felt like the most natural thing in the world. And when he wrapped his arms around her, she snuggled deep into his body and heard his heart beating under her ear. She was where she wanted to be for the rest of her life.

He moved once, reached for something on the night stand, but pulled her back to him when he had it. Before she closed her eyes, knowing that she'd sleep well, he lifted her chin up to look at her.

"I love you." Reid kissed her nose. "And I wanted to know if you'd marry me. I meant to ask you before we went out of doors tonight, but you distracted me."

He slipped the ring over her finger, and then kissed it before she looked at it. "Good Christ. Where did you get this thing?"

He laughed when he held her hand up to look at the ring as it sparkled around the room, the lights from the fireplace making it shine. "It was in the things Phil sent here today. It was in my family's things, but he said that as far as he could tell, my mother never wore it. I think it was my father's mother's. It was in a safety deposit box that hadn't been opened since she passed away when I was little. Phil made sure that I had it for you. So you like it?"

It was yellow gold and old. Four diamonds surrounded the emerald in the middle, and a sapphire, dark blue in brilliance, cradled the tiffany setting of the diamonds. It was simply the most beautiful thing she'd ever seen. The lines of script on the inside were nearly unreadable, but Reid read them to her.

"My love for you is in perpetuity, my life is yours but for the asking." He kissed her again, gently and as if she were fragile. "And it is as true of me to you as it was to the person who wrote this for her."

143

CHAPTER 13

Curt was a wanted man. He read the article twice before he realized that they were talking about him when they said that there was a manhunt out for him, and that he was considered armed and dangerous. First of all, he had no gun or even a paperclip right now, so the armed part was a lie, and how on earth did they even think that he was dangerous? It wasn't his fault that Mike had egged him on.

"You're going to leave here as soon as it's dark." Curt looked up at the man who'd brought him here in the first place. "You're no longer welcome here, and frankly, you're useless to me. I can't even use you as good bait to get Jodie to come to me. She dislikes you as much as I do, and that is a great deal."

"You said you needed my help." Ethan shook his head and moved to the little table that had been set up with their dinner. Curt moved to the table as well and noticed that there was only one place setting, and Ethan was sitting at it.

"I'm afraid you're on your own for your meals as well. I will no longer take the chance of anyone seeing you here with me. I will not go to jail for a moron like you." Curt started to tell him he was no such thing when Ethan continued. "You'll be gone by midnight or I'll make sure that you're permanently gone. As in dead if you don't."

"What the hell am I supposed to do? I gots no money and I gots nothing to drive around in. My brother stole all my money and that's why I killed him." Ethan cut into his steak, and Curt felt his mouth water. "You really ain't going to feed me either?"

"I am not. You're of no use to me, and I should have known that before bringing you here. It is entirely my fault, I will admit that. I should have checked to see what your relationship with that girl was before investing my time into bringing you to my hotel." Ethan took another bite of his steak with a piece of his potato and chewed it completely before continuing. "You'll see that I'm right. Why would you want to endanger me when you've fucked things up so badly for you?"

Curt sat down. He didn't have a clue what the hell he was talking about, and worse yet, he knew he was going to be living on the streets in a few hours. Maybe he could go and find his sister and ask her for help, but he was kind of afraid of her boyfriend and what he might do to him. He looked down at his clothes and wondered if the man would give him something to wear better than this, or would he be expected to be naked again.

"You'll be given a nice set of clothes, but new ones, not mine. I do not want my DNA on any part of you." Curt nodded, not really sure why he thought he'd be giving him his germs, but said nothing. "And I'll give you…I was going to say a hundred dollars, but why would I do that? I'll give you twenty, and hopefully you'll be able to keep that for longer than it takes you to leave this building."

"It wasn't my fault that my brother took my money." Ethan only nodded at him as he bit down into a flaky roll. "Can I just have one more dinner? I swear to you I'll go right afterwards."

Ethan continued to eat his meal, and when he was done, he left nothing on the plate and used his roll to clean up anything that might have been there. Curt tried hard not to hear his belly screaming at him. And when Ethan set the trays on the little trolley and put it in the hallway, Curt thought about attacking him for not even giving a shit he was hungry.

Curt stood up and moved toward the man. He could feel the room tighten as if he was planning to shift, and that confused him enough that he stopped. It was probably the only thing that saved him.

The light that came from Ethan's fingertips startled him for a second. When it touched his arm, it felt as if he'd been branded by a hot iron. Curt started screaming even as he moved toward the man. As soon as he had his fingers around his throat, he was tossed away as if he weighed no more than a loaf of bread. He hit the other wall hard and heard the glass breaking as he slipped to the floor.

Ethan was speaking, but Curt had no idea what he was saying. It wasn't English, he knew that for sure. As soon as he was within touching distance, Curt picked up the leg of the table and slammed it across Ethan's legs, splintering the wood.

It was his only chance of getting out alive. As soon as Ethan hit the floor and tumbled back, Curt ran to the door. He could see the book laying there and grabbed it up too. He had no idea if it was worth anything, but knew that Ethan had been reading it like it was War and Pears or some shit like that. He was out the hall and in the closing elevator when he heard the man scream.

Curt ran out of the hotel just as the police pulled up in front. He was stopped for a second, and he told them that there was a giant snake in the lobby. They let him go and took off running, pulling their guns as he went. He had no idea what they'd been called for, but he was down the street five blocks when he finally slowed. Christ, he was too fat for this shit.

The book was thick, and he nearly trashed it when he realized that it was just a notebook with pages and pages of drawings that made no sense to him and words that looked like they were foreign. But he slipped it into his pant waist band and walked toward the outskirts of town. Maybe he'd try to sell it back to the prick.

Curt walked into the little store at the corner. He didn't have any money, but he thought he could steal something little and maybe feel a little less faint. When he entered, there was a man standing at the register with a gun pointed toward the woman behind the counter. Curt stared at the man for a full five seconds before he pointed the gun at him.

"You, get on the floor." Curt looked down and saw five other people there and two kids. "You deaf? I said get the fuck on the floor."

"I ain't gonna do that. This is all I have to wear and that floor looks nasty." Curt looked at the gunman again and decided he'd had enough people shitting on him for one day and leapt at the man, knocking the gun out of his hand.

148

Before he knew it, he was pounding the guy's head in, and two people were trying to pull him off.

"You got him. I don't think he's going to get up." The man that had been lying on the floor smiled as he helped him stand up. "You saved our lives."

"Nah." Curt felt foolish and tried to go to the door to leave. "I just wanted something to eat. I gotta go now."

The man stopped him and handed him twenty dollars. While Curt was trying to figure out what the catch was, the woman that had been behind the counter started pulling things off the shelves and handed him three bags of food and drinks. He was given seventy more dollars before he told him that he was in trouble with the cops and had to leave, the sirens were already screaming down the street. He slipped out the back door just as one of the cop cars came to a screeching stop. Curt was eating a candy bar and drinking a cold beer before he was a block away.

~~~

Reid watched Jodie carefully. She'd been sitting there staring out the window for nearly an hour now, and he was worried about her. He'd even called Nancy to come over, but she had been in the kitchen cooking since she'd taken one look at Jodie. He started to move to her when Nancy came into the room.

"Come with me." Nancy helped Jodie stand and led her to the kitchen. Reid followed but didn't touch her. Jodie seemed so fragile, and he was afraid for her.

"When did they find him?" Reid looked up at Nancy when Jodie asked. "My brother, when did they find him?"

"They police were at the house and left soon after the

149

two of them were escorted off the property. Dan…he's the cop friend…said that they were pissed off but he didn't think it was directed at each other. Just…well, just you and Austin."

"He killed him. Curt killed Mike for probably no more than the hundred bucks I gave them." Reid had told her about the money being found at the scene. She'd only nodded at him then, and he wondered if she'd remembered he said that. Then she spoke again. "He'll be desperate for money now. Curt never was one to earn a living if stealing it was much easier. I would bet that he wanted the money from Mike and he wouldn't give it to him and attacked him."

Nancy sat a cup of tea in front of an empty seat and handed Jodie a glass of water. He thought the tea was for Nancy, but when someone knocked on the back door, he saw CJ and Austin there. Behind them were all the Force women, including Holly.

Austin motioned for him to go into the other room with him. When he hesitated, Nancy gave him a gentle shove, and he went. As much as he loved this family, he wanted to be near Jodie a good deal more than his alpha right now.

"CJ told me that she and the others are taking her out. She said that it's about time they all got to know her, and this is the perfect day for it." Reid shook his head. "You can tell me no if you want, I don't give a shit. But if you think I'm telling my mate that you said no, you're fucking stupid. She's doing this."

"She's out of it." Austin nodded as he sat down. "I mean she just sat there staring out as if she was…. Fuck I don't know. She didn't take this like I thought she would."

"Because you love your family and she doesn't. That's more than likely what's bothering her. Not that he's dead, but that it doesn't bother her like she thinks it should." Austin leaned back in the chair and pulled out a cigar and put it in his mouth. He'd been doing that since Reid had known him. Never lighting it, just putting it there and savoring it, he supposed. Reid shook his head before he said anything.

"She said she'd marry me." Austin congratulated him. "Now all I have to do is figure out how to contact her father and ask him if I can. Do you suppose Phil can help me?"

"Phil can help you what?" The man in question appeared in the room just as Tristan did. "Something has happened and we need your help. But what did you need?"

Reid looked at Tristan, who looked like he'd been pole axed. Something was up, something major, and Reid would bet his last dollar that it had something to do with Jodie and her family. He started to ask when Jodie came into the room along with CJ.

"Where is he?" She looked at him, then at Tristan. "Where is he? I have to find him before he sells it. You do know that he has the book, right? If he does, he's in danger of Ethan finding him and getting it back."

Book? Reid stood up and started to say something when he was suddenly sitting with his head between his knees. He could hear shouting but not really able to make things out. When he was able to lift his head, Jodie was on her knees in front of him.

"You just got hit with it, didn't you?" She smiled. "I told you last night that it was coming. You had to be careful."

"What the fuck just happened?" He glanced at Austin,

who was being held back by CJ and Tristan. "You morphed into about ten different people, then fainted. What the fuck is going on?"

"He's a shifter. And if I don't miss my guess, which I don't often, he's just had a dose of overload." Phil lifted his head and looked him in the eye. "Do you feel all right?"

"Yeah." Reid stood up and then sat back down. He felt all right but a little dizzy. He looked at Jodie. "She told me last night that once my body accepted the shifter in me that it would have to try it out before it gave me control. I think I have it now."

Reid looked at CJ and thought that would be too freaky and stared at Austin. He knew the moment that he'd become the big man when everyone took a step back. Then he let himself go to become Tristan, then Phil. He settled back into his own body and pulled Jodie to him.

"Mother fuck." Reid nodded at Austin when he spoke. "You can be anyone? I mean that's…you can…mother fuck."

"Yeah, that about covers it." Reid looked around the room. "I'm really sorry that I frightened you all. But Jodie is a shifter that has special abilities, and when we became mates and bonded, then of course I got them as well. She's been showing me other things I can—"

"Don't. Not right now. I just don't think I can handle you shifting into anything like a table or something." Austin raised his hand when Reid started to speak. Poor Austin, he looked slightly green. Austin cleared his throat before he continued. "What is this about a book? He didn't get the one from your mom, did he Phil?"

"No. it's safe." Phil looked at Jodie, then at him before

speaking. "It's a book of spells. Ethan's book as a matter of fact. It's normally protected by the one who owns it. But once it's out of his hands and into someone else's, then... well then it's sort of a beacon to anyone who has a great deal of magic. Like me and Tristan. Like Jodie and Reid now."

"Most people with magic only have a few spells, twenty or so, but not too many past that." Jodie started pacing as she spoke. "A mage has hundreds. Some of them need ingredients to make them work, and others need markings or items not found but made by the mage. They have to write them down, perfect them by putting notes on them. They have to keep meticulous notes on the spells they weave in the event that they may someday have to break the spell."

"And Curt has his book." Jodie nodded at him. "So we have to find him and what? Take it from him before Ethan gets it back? That sounds easy enough."

Tristan was shaking his head, and Reid was afraid of what he was going to tell them when he stood up. He paced the room in the same way his daughter did, and Reid wondered if the two of them knew how much alike they really were.

"Now that Curt has the book, and given the fact that he has a little magic because he can shift, he can use the spells, and the book will become his. If he says one of the incantations or inadvertently messes one up that he might read, then he could do a great deal of harm to the others around him. Or worse yet, to the earth." Phil handed him a sheet of paper as Tristan continued. "That's a mark that will protect the book. But if you turn the sheet over you can see the one that will send the book to anyone who wants it.

You'll notice that there is only the slightest difference in the markings. If he tries it, even messes up one single stroke, everyone who ever had the tiniest bit of magic will have the ability to see that book. It's dangerous to have it out."

"You've touched Curt." Reid looked at Jodie when she suddenly stopped pacing and stared at him. "You hit him at the cemetery and got blood on your hand."

He nodded. There was no mark, of course, that had healed several hours after it happened, but she took his hand into hers and closed her eyes. When she opened them, he could see the fear in her eyes, but instead of asking her what happened, he pulled her close to put his forehead to hers. What she'd found was there for him to see too.

"He's in a warehouse on Denver Street. Third floor in the back. Room thirty-three." Reid watched the man pace. It was weird seeing him like this in her mind, but he knew that they'd need to know everything. Curt appeared to be eating candy bars and drinking beer. "I think he's drunk and the book is—"

"It's in the bed." Jodie pulled back and looked at him as she finished. "You have to go and get it with me. One of us will have to be Ethan and the other will have to get the book. He's already called him to sell it back to him. But Curt's not told him where he's hiding. Ethan isn't going to get the book back."

"No, he won't." Tristan came to stand beside them. He did not look like he was very happy with them. "But you two won't be going after it. I will. I'm the one that needs to do this."

Before Reid could say a word, Tristan was flying back

against the wall and hung there. Jodie stood up, and when Austin made to go toward her, she simply snapped her fingers, and he, too, was against the wall. No one in the room moved, not even when Nancy entered with a tray of cookies and tea.

"You've been being all alpha-like again, haven't you, son?" Nancy sat the tray down and looked at the two men as if seeing them pressed against a wall was an everyday occurrence. "You do know that she's more than likely stronger than both you idiots put together, don't you? And not to mention…. Why don't you try to get free? Both of you, try to break the hold she has on you."

Reid could see them struggling. Jodie didn't move, nor did she gloat that they couldn't get loose. When Tristan started to speak, a strap of tape was over his mouth and the words were cut off.

"I'm a good deal stronger than Ethan as well, though I doubt he knows that right now." Jodie walked toward the two men. "When you agree to shut up and behave yourselves, I'll let you go. Until then, you'll hang here until I come back."

"You should know that when I get down, I'm going to punish you. I'm your alpha." Austin struggled to get free and glared at CJ when she laughed. "What the hell is so funny? I'm your mate. Shouldn't you be at least pissed that she's holding me?"

"You're fucking lucky I don't have you hanging there. I'd have a rope around your neck if you treated me half the way you treat her." CJ looked at Jodie and winked. "You really should let him go. While he can be a bit overbearing at times, he does have a good heart."

155

"He will not tell me what I can and cannot do." Jodie lifted Austin up a little further before she let him go. When he fell to his ass, she said "oops," though Reid didn't think it had been an accident.

They all looked at Tristan, who hadn't been let go. He was glaring at her, but she didn't seem to mind. When she stepped toward her father, she whispered something, and before anyone could say a word, Tristan was gone.

"Jodie?" Phil looked like he was going to say more but only laughed. "I see. Well, that's one way to deal with him."

He'd have to find out later what she'd done to her father. Whatever it was, Phil kept laughing about it off and on for the next hour. The plan was nearly set when he approached Jodie. She nodded once at something Phil said to her, and Tristan was back. If Reid thought he looked pissed before, right now he looked murderous. But he left her alone and sat quietly in the chair where he'd been put when he arrived.

The plan was ready. Was he, he thought? Not really, but if she said it would work, then he was willing to give it a try. Christ, he hoped he didn't fuck up.

CHAPTER 14

Curt looked out the window for the tenth time in as many minutes. Where the hell was he? And where the hell was his money? Curt glanced out again when he heard something and sneered at the five or six little boys playing in the yard beyond the building he was in.

Ethan had been livid, and Curt had almost run out of quarters when he'd had to call him back several times. The payphone a mile from where he was staying was the only one he'd seen all day and frankly, if asked, he would have said that they didn't exist anymore. Looking out the window again, he moved to the pallet he'd been sleeping on when he'd gotten there. The newspaper with his picture on the front page still scared him when he looked at it.

Murder, it said. He was wanted in connection with the murder of his brother, and there were questions about his father's death as well. Curt hadn't been able to go out but once since this whole thing had started, and that time nearly got caught. Christ, did everyone want to be mean to him?

Curt had been trying to find someone to rob a store. He didn't want them to really do it, but he wanted someone to rob a place so that he could go in and save the day again.

When it had happened the other day, he'd been so happy for the entire day, feeling good that people had looked up to him. He wanted it again. But that wasn't going to happen now.

The first person he'd approached had told him to fuck off. Curt was nearly ready to attack the man when he turned suddenly and laughed. Curt didn't know what to think so took two steps back when the man had reached into his pants. He nearly wet himself in relief when all he pulled out was a newspaper.

"This is you." Curt looked at the picture of himself that was on the front page and then back at the man when he laughed again. "I got me a real live murderer here and didn't even know it. They's offering a reward for you to be bringed in. I think I might just go and collect it."

Curt took off running. He wanted to shift, but knew that if he tore his clothes up this time, he was fucked. He didn't have anything but the clothes on his back right now. Instead, he ran and hid until it was dark and then moved to his place, looking over his shoulder the entire time.

A car pulled up in front of the building, and he got up to see. There was a man standing next to the back door, and when he opened it and helped someone out, Curt let go of the breath he'd been holding. Finally, Ethan was there to pay him off.

It took him forever, it seemed like, to get to his floor, and Curt stilled when he heard voices. Not just Ethan's but someone else, a woman. He started to hide when a loud punching knock sounded at the door. Curt looked in the peep hole and saw just Ethan there.

158

"Well, moron, you going to let me in or are we going to stand here playing peek-a-boo all night?" Curt didn't understand and frowned. Why would he want to play a child's game? "Open the fucking door, you moron."

Curt pulled the chain loose and stepped back. The man simply stood there, and Curt had an overwhelming feeling that he was going to die. Before he could slam the door in his face, Ethan asked him if he was going to invite him in.

"Yeah, sure. Won't you come in?" Ethan moved into the room like he owned it. He looked around the shabby place like he expected something to jump out at him. Curt wanted to tell him that all the rats had run off the minute he'd moved in, but didn't. Instead, he stared at the man.

"You have my book?" Curt nodded and continued to stare. "Well?"

Curtis knew that he was on the slow side. He'd never finished high school, had barely finished middle school, for that matter, and could only read at a third grade level, but Ethan was standing there, looking at him as if he didn't have the smarts to even lace up his shoes. He looked down at them now.

Of course, they were untied and worse yet, his socks didn't match. Curt felt anger surge over him as Ethan started to pat his foot. His mother had done that, and he'd never understood how it could tell you so much without saying a word.

"I want my money." Ethan reached into his pocket and pulled out a brown envelope. It looked thick enough to have the five thousand dollars in it, but what would he know? He'd never seen that much money at once in his life. Just

159

as he was reaching for it another knock sounded at the door.

Just as he turned to answer it, he felt a tightening in the room. Curt glanced back at Ethan, and he was suddenly gone. In his place was an eddy of air that stirred the dust. He opened the door to find him standing outside again.

"What the fuck are you doing? I don't gots all day for you to be playing around." Curt giggled when he finally got the peek-a-boo reference. "You think I wanna play games with you?"

"What the hell are you talking about? Give me my book and let's get this over with." Curt invited him in again and watched as the man stomped in but said nothing. "Where is it?"

"I gots it hidden. You won't find it until I say so." Curt was momentarily distracted when he saw a movement out of the corner of his eye and stared at it. Ethan slapped him.

"Are you normally this stupid or is it that you think this will get you out of giving me what you stole from me? I assure you that it won't." Curt watched as the shape he'd seen seemed to appear then disappear twice before he realized who it was.

"Jodie? What the hell are you doing here?" Ethan turned just as his sister materialized fully. She smiled as she pulled the book he'd been going to sell to Ethan from his hidey-hole and put it into her shirt. She was gone before either of them could move.

"How the hell did she do that?" Curt looked at Ethan when he growled. "Did you see her when you comed in the first time? Or did you bring her with you?"

"The first time?" Ethan took a step toward the bed when

he was suddenly gone as well. Curt wasn't sure what was going on, but he leapt for the door to get out of his room. Something was taking people, he just knew it. And he wasn't going wherever the others had gone. Standing in the hallway looking into the room he heard the car downstairs start up and move away. It wasn't until he could hear the kids again that he realized the envelope that the first Ethan had brought was still lying in the middle of the floor. He made his way back into the room cautiously and picked it up.

"Mother fuck." There wasn't anything in the thing but slips of paper. And on each one was the single word "murderer." Curt dropped it all and stepped back. The sirens sounding outside were almost a welcome relief. When the cops came into his room, he was nearly begging them to take him.

"Careful, this here room will take you away if you don't watch it. Took Jodie away and Ethan too." The cops didn't look all that impressed with him so he tried again. "You should have seen the first Ethan. He was driving a limo and had on a suit. The second one had on a pair of neat-o pants that seemed to be made of something shiny and a long robe."

He was being put into a cruiser when he realized that he was in big trouble. They were reading him his rights and saying something about murder. He tried to tell them it was Jodie's fault he'd kill Mike, and that when he poisoned his dad, it was because he wanted to sell the land. The police nodded as if they understood, and Curt felt much better. Perhaps he wasn't in as much trouble as he'd thought.

~~~

Jodie looked at each page before going to the next. It

161

was thick with information and some of it she could only guess what he'd needed the spell for. When Reid came into the room, she looked up at him as he leaned against the doorjamb. She smiled when he did.

"They haven't found Ethan yet. Tristan is pissed, of course, but he's calming a little. Phil is having fun at his expense, which, needless to say, isn't making the other vampire any happier. And Austin is in our kitchen wanting to speak to you." Reid closed the door behind him when he came fully into the room. "He looks like he's been told he can't have any more cookies today."

"CJ reached out to me just now. She and Austin have had it out, she said. I'm not sure what that means to them, but she asked me to cut him some slack. He's trying to be a good guy about this." She lifted her legs off the couch when he sat next to her. Then he pulled them across his lap. "I thought the big bad alpha wanted to talk to me."

"He does, but I think he can stew for a bit." Reid started to massage her calves. She wanted to beg him to keep it up, but he stilled and looked at her. "Curt has been arrested. They've charged him with first degree murder as well as they are looking into the death of your father. He admitted to that as they took him in. Told them it was your fault apparently. That you'd driven him to it."

"He would think that. And I figured that he'd be too stupid to keep his mouth shut." She waited for him to say more, but when he didn't, she continued, "I've been looking at Ethan's book. He wasn't so much powerful as he was stupid. He had a spell here that would reverse the effects of graying hair. When I thought about it, I noticed that he had

KATHI S. BARTON

more when he showed up at the warehouse than he did when he first attacked me."

"He'll be desperate now." Jodie nodded, knowing that he was talking about Ethan. "I don't think he'll be so nice when he finds you this time. He will outright kill you, I think."

"He'll try." Reid started to massage her leg again. She watched him, knowing that he had something on his mind, but what, she didn't know. And she wouldn't pry either. She didn't want to do that unless it was necessary. He looked at her, and she knew that he'd come to a great decision. One she didn't think she'd like.

"I'd very much like for you to listen to me before you get pissed. All right?" She nodded. "I know that you're very strong and well-equipped to handle this guy. I know that in my head. But my heart tells me that if you do this and I can't protect you, somehow you're going to get hurt. And that I can't stand. He's not going to stop until he has you now. Ethan knows you have his book, and worse yet, he thinks that killing you will give him whatever you have too."

She started to point out he would have it, but didn't think he'd handle that so well. Instead, she stood up and stared down at him. The man simply made her heart beat a little faster and her body hum with need. When he growled low, she knew that he'd felt her desire for him.

"Did you know that with this book I can do whatever he could do?" She opened it to a random page and said the incantation there and watched as the room flooded with light even though it was nearly dark. "That was for a vampire. In the event that he was caught unawares and needed a quick

163

getaway."

"The sun light would kill them." She nodded at his statement. "And in that book of evilness, is there anything that will make you one hundred percent safe from him?"

"Yes and no." She turned the pages to a marking. It was a circle with several other markings within it. Jodie showed it to him. "We need to get this put at the windows and doors of this house. It will ward off every species that comes within ten miles of here that we're very strong."

"I can do that. If I could, I'd like to suggest that all the other members of this family use it as well." She nodded and put out her hand. She'd already made five of them to hang in the windows of this floor. Reid told her he'd give them to each Force, including Phil.

"There's something else." She didn't want to tell him this, so she suggested they go to the kitchen. He didn't move at first, but finally stood and went with her. Austin was sitting at the table on his cell phone. When they sat across from him, he closed it with a snap.

"I'm sorry." She nodded and smiled at him. "I was an overbearing ass, and my wife told me that if she…. She said that it's small wonder that you didn't put a hex on me or something."

"I couldn't do that before." He glanced at the book, then looked at her again. "Yes, there is one here in. It will make you change to wolf and stay that way. Also you should know that according to the notes in the margins, Ethan has been practicing on your kind for a very long time."

"Christ." Austin got up and opened a cabinet that she'd never noticed before. He pulled out a bottle of Johnny

Walker Blue and then three glasses. He poured three nearly full tumblers full of the nearly two hundred and fifty dollar label before he sat down. Austin drained his glass before he looked at her while pouring more into his glass.

His body said he was prepared for whatever she told him, but his face said he didn't want to know. Then she took a sip of the finest Scotch she'd ever tasted and started.

"There are over two hundred names in this book of people that had served him. Most of them were adults, but a few, quite a few, were children. He also tried his best to breed them into other beings. Cross breeding is high on his list of experiments." Austin took another healthy drink. "You're going to get drunk."

"No, sadly, I can't, but it can make me feel good for a few moments." He looked at Reid. "I'll replace this. I had no idea you drank."

Reid shook his head and smiled. "It sort of came with the house. I would imagine Tristan had a hand in it being here. But this deserves it I think."

Austin looked at her again and she nodded before telling him more. "About ten years ago he found that he could get couples, mates, to breed him a child, and he'd take it from the womb and dice it. After a few weeks, he'd try something more with another child, then another. But nothing was working the way he wanted. He hoped to use the child as a way to prolong his life. All it did was it managed to get him was a pack of wolves after him. He is wanted in three different packs across the country."

"I'll let them know he's here if you have the names." She told him she did. "I know that you're working up to

165

something here. And while under normal circumstances I'd tell you to get to the point, I don't want it yet. Is there something else you can tell me that will work me up to the horror I know you're keeping from me?"

"Five years ago he was working in a lab with a vampire. His name isn't mentioned, but that's not unusual. To keep yourself safe you'd never give anyone your name in his line of business." Austin started to reach for the bottle again, but she moved it from him. "Pay attention. You have to know this so it can save your life."

"He knew who we are. The sick bastard wants some of my pack now, doesn't he?" Jodie waited to see if he'd get it, and when he did, she felt sorry for him. "Christ, he's got some of them now. Where? Do you know?"

She pushed the book toward him, and he backed from it. Jodie knew how he felt. Touching the book somehow made what was in it seem so much more real. When he looked down at the address then up at her, she could see the pain in his eyes.

"I own this building. It's been sitting empty for about nine years now. Are you saying that he's been using it all along?" She nodded. "Christ, what do I do to get him out?"

"It's done." He nodded and got up to pace. "Tristan contacted me earlier while I was reading this. I told him what was happening, and he said he'd take care of it. But he asks that you stay away for now. There is a matter of you not knowing so that you can't get into trouble."

"But I do now." The phone rang and Reid went to answer it. "Is that them? Are the police telling me what they've found?"

166

"Yes." She watched him age several years as he sat at the table. She had a feeling he was talking to his mate, and when CJ knocked on the door while he was on the phone with the police, she knew it. Jodie sat down with Reid as CJ and Austin tried to calm each other. Jodie had one more thing to tell him, and she dreaded this most of all.

CHAPTER 15

Austin walked around the building with the police. The Feds had been called in as well, and there were all kinds of news crews and television station vans around the yellow tape too. He didn't want anyone here but knew that this was as necessary as breathing. He looked over at Phil, who had insisted on coming with him.

"They're going to drag this out for months. You know that, right?" Phil nodded but said nothing. "I told CJ that I didn't want her here, but I wish she was."

"I had her come down in another car. She's at the hotel. Holly is there as well. I knew this was going to be bad." Phil handed him a cell phone. "It's Jodie. She said she needs to tell you something."

Austin didn't want to take the phone. He didn't want to talk to her either. She had brought this to him, and he wasn't all that sure he could handle much more. There were over two hundred files in the cabinets inside the office they'd found, and there were only sixteen bodies. They'd been dead for about a week, the coroner had told him. He put the phone to his ear.

"Stand in front of the building so that the stairs are dead

center to you." He moved to where she'd told him before asking what for. "See the upper window on the left? There is a curtain in front of it."

"I see it." It was a very small window in comparison to the other ones, and while he watched, the curtain moved. "Jodie, is there someone up there?"

"Yes. The doctors of this place. Or whatever they were calling themselves. You need to find them and let me find you. They'll tell me where the other people are." He could feel her excitement. "I think there are at least fifty if not a few more others alive and they will know where they are."

Austin moved toward the building and was only stopped once. Phil ran interference with him a couple of more times until he and Phil were standing before the long hall that Jodie had led them to. He asked her what she wanted him to do now, but she didn't answer. Suddenly she was standing in front of him.

"I couldn't find it on the maps. You had to lead me there." She started down the hall only to stop when he touched her arm. She looked at him, and he knew that whoever was on the other side wasn't going to live long if they didn't give her the answers she wanted. He let her go on following right behind her.

The door opened about three feet before she got to it. There were nine men and women in the room, and all of them were huddled in the corner away from the window. Austin could almost feel sorry for them if he didn't know that they'd done the monstrous things that had been done to the beings downstairs.

The blast of light from her fingertips had one man lying

dead. His head had been taken from his body and no blood spilled onto the floor. Austin knew that whatever it was she'd hit him with had been hot, as it had cauterized the flesh almost as soon as she'd cut him.

"Where are they?" No one moved, and she killed another one. This woman had her heart torn from her chest without anyone touching her. Austin watched as it continued to beat for several seconds after it lay beside her. "I won't ask twice. Someone had better fucking tell me what I want to know or I'll kill you all."

"They're at the farm." The man who spoke up cringed when she took a step toward him. "Please don't kill me. Please. If I take you there, will you please not kill me?"

"I'm not making any promises." He paled even more as Jodie spoke. "Close your eyes and think of the place."

The man begged her again as she raised her hand up. Austin watched as the man's eyes snapped closed and Jodie nodded. Before he could ask her where it was, they were standing in front of a large barn that smelled of antiseptic, and he could hear the hum of something powerful running.

"They're in here?" Jodie nodded but held him back. "I need to see if any of them are alive."

"They aren't." Austin looked at the barn, then at her. "They stored them here until they could get someone out here to use the backhoe to bury them. There are way more in here than at the lab. The living ones are in there." She nodded to the house beyond them.

"I'll have to call in...." He looked at her when she started to shake her head. "They might need my help. I have to do something."

"Do you own this farm?" He tried to think if he did or not and realized that he didn't. "Then how will you explain that you knew they were here?"

"Then what the fuck would you have me do? Leave them there on the off chance that someone might think to look here? Hope to Christ that there's a hint of it at the lab?" He pushed her away from him and started for the house. She was standing in front of him before he could step onto the porch. "I can't leave them there."

"This is where he tried to kill me." He looked at the house, then at her again. "Ethan brought me here to kill me so that he could have what I am. I know who owns this. I can get them help today, but you have to trust me."

Austin knew he had no choice. It was trust her or have the police wonder how he knew as much as he did. Nodding once, he knew that she'd brought them back to his building again as soon as he opened his eyes. They were back again in front of the lab, and he looked at her.

"They're dead. I wasn't going to let them poison the system with their information. Ethan had told them that they'd be rescued if they were ever caught. Maybe he would have and maybe not, but I couldn't take the chance." Austin didn't speak to her the rest of the time they were at the site. He knew in some way she was right, but right now all he could think about was how cold she was. She'd killed those people without a moment's hesitation. The next time he thought about her she was gone and Reid was talking to Phil. He approached the man with a heavy heart.

"She's with CJ and the others." Austin didn't ask him, but Reid told him all the same. "When this is over, she wants

172

to talk to you. She said it's important."

"All right." Austin waited for the officer to walk away before he asked Reid about the barn. "Did she find someone to go there? She said she would."

"The police showed up about ten minutes ago. The owners had gone out to mow the lawn and to check the house out with the thoughts of selling the land. They walked into the house and found fifty six men, women, and children huddled in rags nearly starved to death. They're being treated now." Austin felt as if a burden had been lifted from his shoulders. When Reid started to walk away, he stopped him and asked him to thank Jodie.

Reid stared hard at him. Austin had a feeling that he was thinking hard on whether or not to hit him when he finally nodded. This time when he walked away, Austin let him and looked at Phil for answers.

"She's leaving him. First thing after Ethan is caught." Austin looked at Reid before looking back at Phil as he continued. "I've been asked to sell the house and pay off his student loans. I don't know what he's planning to do, but I don't think he's going to be able to follow her."

"Why not?" Phil shrugged, and Austin tried again. "Where does she think she's going without him?"

"With her father." Austin didn't know what that meant, but before he could ask for clarification, an officer asked him if he could come with him. He was shown the room where the doctors had been, and the room was now empty of everything, including the bodies.

"Do you know what this room was for, sir?" Austin told him he didn't. "Then do you know someone who might? I know you haven't been here in years, you told us that, but someone has been using this place and we wondered if you knew who."

"I'm sorry, I don't." Austin looked around the room again and saw the book just behind some papers. He didn't move toward it but in the general area. When the officer turned to talk to someone else, he slipped the book in his coat and waited for the police to take him down. He handed the book to Phil when he was alone with him.

"She left the book there." Phil opened it, and a sheet of paper fell out. He picked it up and handed it to him. It was from Jodie.

> *"No one will question you about this book. If you'd be so kind as to give it to Mrs. Campbell, I'm sure she'll know what to do with it. Ethan won't have any use for it from now on."*

Christ, she was going after him. Austin handed the note to Phil as he moved to find Reid. He reached for CJ at the same time.

"Is Jodie still with you?" She told him she'd never been there. *"Christ, she's going after Ethan on her own. Mother fuck, that girl is driving me nuts."*

Austin found Reid ten minutes later. He was working with the medics in taking out the bodies and making notes on how they were murdered. Austin had forgotten that Reid was a doctor and was proud of him for helping out. But he asked to speak to him privately.

"Do you know where Jodie is?" Reid started to walk

away, but Austin stopped him. "I think she's gone after Ethan on her own."

Without turning around to look at him, Reid answered. "She has. And I'm to stay away because she said you'd never forgive her if anything happened to me. I argued with her, but after seeing the way you treated her here, I think she's right."

"I never meant to…I was overwhelmed. She killed those people without a thought to—"

Reid turned to look at him then. "You think so? You think she killed those doctors without a thought to what they'd done to the hundreds of people we're pulling out? You think that she just murdered them, cut their life short without thinking about the fact that they might have families, children of their own?" Reid turned back and faced the hundreds of body bags that were already lined up in the yard. "Yeah, she thought about it as much as these people did when they did this."

Reid walked away, and Austin dropped to his knees. He was still sitting that way when Tristan came to him. There was nothing this man could say to him that wouldn't hurt him more. He looked up at him.

"Jolene has been captured by Ethan. He said he'd return her in pieces if we didn't give him the book. She told me if we did, then you might as well kill your family now because he's going to when he gets it." Austin stood up with his help.

"We have to get her." Tristan nodded but he said nothing to him. "I'm going to find her, save her stupid ass, then I'm going to kick her butt all over the place for making me this nuts."

175

Austin found Reid again and told him what had happened with the help of Tristan. They were moving toward their cars when Hope was suddenly there. She looked like she'd been through hell. Austin reached for her as she stumbled.

"Ethan just contacted me. He knows I have the Book of Life. He said that he also has the girl. I'm assuming he means Jodie?" They nodded, and Hope put her hands on Reid's cheeks as she looked him in the eyes. "She's with child. I was going to tell you when this was over, but she must have gone into heat right after I repaired the damage. I'm so sorry, Reid, but when he sent me her blood, I could smell it on her."

"Christ." Austin had to help Reid to his car. He was worried about him all the way to the hotel, and when they entered the room where the women were, he nearly snarled at him to sit down when he stood up.

"I'm going after her." Reid moved to the door and stopped when his mom hit him in the forehead with her spoon. "I'm not in the mood for you to think—"

"I got news for you young man. I'm not in the mood either. But if you think I'm going to let you go off halfcocked after her, I might just use this spoon in another part of your body that might feel a good deal more painful." When Reid growled, so did his mom. Reid backed up but didn't look happy about it. "Now then, what do we know, and how do we get her back?"

"Ethan contacted me about an hour ago. He said that he has her and will return her when he gets his book back. According to him, there are ways for him to tell if we've made copies of it." Tristan shrugged. "I doubt that it's true.

176

I've looked the book over, and as far as I can tell the only spell on it is the one that I put on it years ago."

"And what sort of spell is that?" Tristan flushed, and Austin quirked a brow at him. This was going to be good. "Tristan, what is it?"

"He won't be able to make any spell or incantation work so long as its black magic used to reproduce. He can do anything he wants using white, but the black won't let him get anyone pregnant or even himself have a child so long as he uses it." Tristan shook his head. "I should have simply made it so the book wouldn't open for him. That would have worked better."

"You can put me in the book." Everyone turned to look at Reid when he spoke. "Jodie told me that there was a spell in the book that could put a person in it. Like on a page. As soon as the book is opened, the person slips out and becomes solid again. She said that he made it up so that he could hide in other people's luggage to travel so he'd not have to pay for it. It also got him around without anyone finding him."

"You want us to use one of his spells to put you into a book that killed hundreds of people. For what? Do you plan to try and stop him?" Austin shook his head as he continued. "No, I don't think so. We'll figure out a way to find her that doesn't involve magic."

"Where is it in the book? Do you remember?" Austin watched as he was completely ignored, and Tristan and Reid looked over the book. Hope sat next to him on the sofa and patted his hand.

"Sometimes it's better to be a leader by letting others do the thinking." He looked at her, wanting to ask her what the

177

hell she was talking about. But she smiled. "He knows what he's doing. Both of them do. Reid may not know it, but he has the power to move mountains, and Tristan is the perfect man to show him how."

"He might get hurt." She nodded and watched him. "I guess I could get hurt simply by walking to the bedroom, but this is magic we're talking about. Dark magic that gets people killed."

"I'm sure he knows that. More than you do, I would imagine. But she's his mate. Would you do no less for your own mate? Or your children?" He wouldn't, but before he could tell her it wasn't the same, she continued. "He's going to be called to help in a great deal more than this in the coming years. Jodie works for all kinds of people and with his help and stability she'll be much safer. As a doctor, he'll see things long before any of us do with her and as her mate, he'll be able to make sure she takes the time she needs. He won't have to boss her like some people I know, either."

Austin knew that he'd been rough on the girl. CJ had pointed it out to him several times over the past few weeks. And maybe he'd been the one to drive her to find Ethan, too, by pissing her off one too many times at the lab. He looked around the room, wondering if he'd do the same if it were his mate, and knew without a doubt that he would. He had, as a matter of fact. When Reid started to argue with Tristan about something, he walked to the two men.

"I think Reid is right. He has more juice than any of us, and he'd be better equipped to handle something if it went wrong." He looked at the younger man. "I think if we didn't allow him to do this, he'd figure out a different way to get

178

her back that might get them both hurt. I say we do what he needs and protect him as best we can."

Phil patted him on the back, and Austin knew that he'd made the right decision. It wasn't what he wanted but knew that it was right. As soon as the plan started to be put into place, he was more and more proud of the young man. Reid had grown up over the last few years.

He had been such a scrawny kid when he and CJ had first found him and his brother. The kid had even tried to take him on and would have, too, getting himself killed if CJ hadn't walked up to him and slapped him right across the face. He could still hear her question to him as if it were just this morning.

They'd been shopping at this shop she loved. He'd only just figured out that he loved her, and she looked at the boys out in the yard when he'd told her to go to the rig. CJ shoved the things they'd picked out into his arms. She walked straight to the boy and his friends and smacked the taller one across the mouth. Austin started cussing right behind her. The kid looked at her while he rubbed his mouth.

"What the fuck was that for?" the kid next to him snarled with a step toward her. She drew back and slapped him too.

"You'll watch your mouth, young man." She looked at the kid she'd slapped first. "Did that hurt?"

"Yeah, you want me to show you?" She drew back her hand again, and he took a step back. "Are you nuts?"

"So it hurt? Good. Now tell me, what do you think that the man behind me would have done to you? Less? More?" Austin was right behind her, but he didn't say anything. "I want you to take a good look at him and tell me truthfully what you think would have happened."

The boy looked over her shoulder and then took a step back. "He probably would have killed me."

"Austin?" Austin had nodded at the boy when she'd said his name. He'd seen no reason to lie or sugar coat it.

"Oh yeah, he'd be a dead pup. Might still be if he doesn't show my mate more respect." After finding out as much as he could on the boys and sending them on to Vegas for the wedding, Austin had never been happier that they'd taken them in. And more so now. This young man was going to get his mate back and conquer whatever bad news was going on with the mage too. Austin knew he would as surely as he was standing there.

CHAPTER 16

Jodie moved her arms, trying to stretch them so that they didn't hurt as much. She laughed softly. She wasn't sure she'd ever hurt less no matter what she did to improve how she was standing here. Waiting was not one of her better points. And she'd been waiting for over three hours.

A movement in front of her had her tensing to a more defensive position and listening for whoever came in. It was Ethan again, and this time he was alone. The last time he'd come to her he'd tried to get his flunky to subdue her, but she'd managed to break his neck. Quick work of it too.

Watching from beneath her lashes, she saw him moving around the room and to the tables that had been set up. She'd have to do something with them the next time he was gone, and decided that a nice little meltdown was just the thing. A sound like a bell going off had her thinking it was a timer, but she realized it was a door bell. A sick one too if the noise it made the second time was any indication. When he left the room, she looked around.

The beakers exploded. She didn't waste any time in wondering if the gasses would harm her. Killing this bastard was high on her list of last things to do before she went to

181

live with her father.

The books were torched. She didn't know what they were, but the smoke was enough to let her know that they were old books and some of them had leather for covers. By the time Ethan returned, she'd pretty much destroyed the room.

He stood staring at the damage before turning to her. The bindings at her arms suddenly let go, and she staggered slightly when her feet touched the floor. He didn't move toward her, but she could see the anger in the set of his face.

"You think you can stop me?" She shrugged, and he glared at her. "Tell me your name. I know it's not that ridiculous name your so-called brother called you. I tried to summon you three times and you never came. What is it?"

"Never going to happen." He took a step toward her, and she lifted her hand and tossed him across the room. That's when she noticed that he had the book. "You think that's going to save you from me? Think again, dickweed. I'm a good deal stronger than I was when we met the last time."

"You think so? Well so am I. I've been coming up with some spells that will take you and that fucking family of dogs you live with out of the picture. And that man too, the vampire. I'm going to enjoy tearing him apart." Jodie laughed. If he was talking about Tristan, he was insane. Even Phil could take him on if need be. The touch of her mind had her still.

"You should have him open the book. We've gone to a great deal of trouble to get Reid to you. The very least you can do is bring him out to play." She ignored Hope for trying to think why they'd do something so stupid as to send in

182

Reid. *"Like we could have stopped him. The young pup was going to do it whether we wanted him to or not."*

"And you being this bad assed vampire you couldn't stop him I suppose." Jodie felt her laughter. *"You bitch. If he gets hurt I'm going to hunt you down."*

"In order to do that you're going to have to get out of this alive. Where are you anyway?" Jodie told Hope Campbell to fuck off. *"Tisk tisk, such language. What will the women's club think of you if you say that to them?"*

"Like I give a shit. How do I get Reid back to you? And don't tell me the wrong spell. I've been unraveling them for months so I know what you're telling me." Hope laughed. *"I'm not in the best of humor here. Tell me."*

"Whatever are you doing?" She'd forgotten about Ethan while talking to Hope. "You can't be talking to any of the wolves. This room is lined with steel and your link to him is cut off." Jodie cleared the table with the book on it with her mind and watched as Ethan tried not to get cut by flying glass. "Stop that right now. Damn it all to hell, I don't have time to start over."

The table bent under her command, the book skittered across the room and under a shelf. She started to tell Hope that she'd taken care of the book when Ethan pulled it out and opened it. Jodie closed her eyes as the bright light nearly knocked her back.

Reid looked good enough to eat. She took a step back when he looked at her. Someone had given him some powerful magic. His eyes glowed with it. When he leaned against the wall she was confused and so, apparently, was Ethan.

"You're just going to let me kill her?" Reid laughed, throwing back his head with it. She had to smile. Christ, the man could make her insides warm with that laugh. She looked at Ethan when he started cursing. "What the hell are you doing here? Who sent you?"

"I think we should break this down one question at a time. Number one. Am I going to let you kill her? No. First of all, you won't be able to because I'm pretty sure she's going to kill you anyway. Secondly, I thought it'd be fun to watch my mate kick someone else's ass for a change. Her brother wasn't much of a challenge." Reid grinned as he continued. "Second one. What am I doing here? Okay, I sort of jumped the gun on that one. I'm here to watch her—"

"Quiet." Spittle dripped from Ethan's lips as he stood there. He was mad, she knew that, but the extent of his madness was more than she'd thought. She turned to Reid to tell him to leave before he got hurt when she noticed that he had the book. And as suddenly as it was in his hand, it was gone.

"You're father taught me that one. He said that it will be safe until I bring it back." He sent her his love, bathing her in it. *"Let's take care of this fucking idiot and go home. I'd very much like to take you to bed and have my way with you several times over."*

"You do know that I'm pissed that you're here, right? You should be with your family. And I with mine." He shook his head at her, but before either of them could comment, Ethan came at her.

~~~

Reid held onto the table with all he was. Nothing he

184

wanted in this world right now was more important than the woman who now fought for both of them. He was calming his wolf, telling him that he'd have her as soon as she was finished, when Ethan hit the wall again.

"You're nothing but a lazy prick." Ethan spit blood out and it landed on the floor between them. "I thought wolves were supposed to be protective of their females. Are you going to just let me keep at her without raising a finger?"

Reid looked at Jodie. Other than a little blood on her lip, she didn't look as if she'd been hurt at all. He knew that she'd been hit a few times—every part of his heart had felt each blow—but she was standing on her own and looked to be ready for another round with the mage. Her magic was more than he'd bargained for.

"I think she's doing a good job on her own. Besides, as badly as she's kicking your ass, I don't want to get in her way." Reid gripped tighter on the table and lied to the man. "I'm sort of bored with this shit anyway. Maybe I'll just go home and wait for her."

The low growl didn't bother him. Nor did it give him any pause when the mage stood up. He'd been going at this for such a short time, and Reid didn't know how much more he could take of simply sitting by. But when Ethan moved toward him, Reid lifted his hand and whispered the four words that he'd read in the book of spells.

He knew it would stop the mage. But that wasn't all it did. He froze—ice crystalized around his body so quickly that the room chilled by several degrees. All that moved was his eyes, and they looked to be full of terror. Reid moved to Jodie to pull her into his arms.

"You okay?" She nodded and looked up at him. He kissed her gently on the lips, careful of the small cut there. When she opened her mouth under his, he couldn't have resisted her any more than he could stop breathing. Christ, she tasted delicious.

Forgetting about the man in the room with them, he lifted her up and took her to the nearest wall. Her legs wrapping around him had him rocking hard into her even as she licked a path from his ear to his throat. When she bit into him, Reid roared out, his entire body primed to come.

"I want you." She moaned as she drank from him. "Christ, I need to be inside of you. He cupped her breast in his palm and pulled at her nipple. When she lifted her head from his throat, he took her mouth again, tasting his blood on her mouth. He was ready to tear her clothes off her when he felt someone else in the room. Reid turned slightly to see Tristan there.

"You should probably finish this somewhere else." Reid nodded at the vampire. "But I was wondering if I might use your lovely mate for a few minutes. There is some unfinished things here we have to do."

Jodie dropped her feet to the floor, and Reid stepped back. He didn't turn as yet. His cock was painfully swollen, and he wanted to finish what they'd started. Jodie stepped around him, giggling, and he felt his heart take a wonderful leap.

Tristan had his back to him when he turned. Reid was glad for that. When Jodie walked up beside her father, Tristan wrapped his arm around her and kissed her forehead. Reid felt his wolf stir, but he didn't get pissy. Not yet at least.

"Hello, Ethan Thomas Randolph." The mage blinked several times, and fear replaced the hatred that had been there before. "Oh, I'm sorry. Let me have her make it so you can speak if you'd like."

Jodie turned to him, and he had to smile. Tristan hadn't expected him to be able to do that apparently. But to only remove only a portion of the ice he did need help. Jodie whispered the incantation into his ear, and he repeated it softly. The ice crumbled away so that only Ethan's head was cleared.

"There we go. Now, as I was saying. You've yet to figure out who I am, have you?" Tristan tisked several times. "And I gave you so many clues. You killed my mate, nearly killed me, and now you've tried to kill this woman and her mate. You don't have a very good track record regarding my family, do you?"

"Family? Not possible. If I killed your mate, you'd not have children. Especially none as old as her." Ethan looked at him. "And how is it possible that he had magic? He's nothing more than a wolf, and not a very strong one either."

"Really?" Tristan turned to look at him before turning back to Ethan. "It would seem that you are incorrect. You are held in a pretty powerful spell. Or did you want me to believe that you did this for me?"

Ethan growled. Reid didn't know what was going on, but he had a feeling that it wasn't going to end well for the mage. Reid took a step forward and brought his body up against Jodie's. When she leaned back on him, he wrapped his arms around her waist, careful not to block her arms.

"I digress. This is my daughter; you killed her mother

187

when she was but a babe. I had been buried deep below the earth, healing from an injury that you gave me. Nearly killed me then, but that's not what drove me to find you. You took away my being able to watch my daughter blossom into a beautiful woman. And for that…." Tristan lifted his hand and bright lights danced from his fingertips. "And for that you should die."

The lights stopped, and Tristan stepped back. Reid started to as well, but Jodie put her hand on his arms around her and took a step forward. As soon as he realized what was going to happen, he held her tighter. She was going to kill him, and when she did, his power would come to her.

The words whispered seemed to tighten the room. The quicker she said them, the more Ethan struggled against his bonds. When the ice started to crack and craze, Reid touched the ice and strengthened it. When Ethan started screaming, Reid closed his eyes.

It was over in seconds.

"You should probably go now." Reid opened his eyes to look at Jodie when she spoke. "I'm going to help my father clean up here, then we'll be leaving."

At first he was pissed off. She really was going to leave him. Then he looked at her, really looked. She was hurting. And he knew who'd done this to her. Austin was going to pay for this.

"I'm not going anywhere." He felt his head start to feel a little light and reached out for something to hold onto. "You and I are mates, and we're not going to be parted."

"What's wrong?" Her voice seemed to fade in and out from shouting so loudly that he felt as if she were in his head to barely a whisper. When his knees started to buckle, he reached out blindly and felt her grab him. Jodie was screaming for him, but he didn't know what she wanted. Blinding pain took his breath away, and his belly started to lurch. He was going to be sick. Throwing up made his throat burn. Then he started to fade out. Letting himself freefall into the darkness, he heard his wolf sigh. The poor thing was sick too.

Curling up into a ball on the bed, he laid as still as he could when he woke up. He wasn't in so much pain that he wanted to die from it now, but he did still feel like shit. His belly was churning in a way that had him think of a nasty sea voyage, and that made him feel worse. Reid looked up at her when she said his name.

"You're home." He nodded and kissed her hand when she ran it over his face. "You need a bath too. You smell like a wet dog."

Reid growled at her, and she laughed. He moved his head slowly so that he could watch her as she got off the bed. She was wearing one of his shirts again and no pants. His cock jumped to attention.

"Come here." She turned to look at him over her shoulder. "Come here and let me fuck you."

Her giggle made him smile, but he still wanted her. When she stood in front of the window in their bedroom, he could see that she wasn't wearing a bra, and he hoped to Christ she didn't have any panties either. He needed her right now.

"I think you're still too weak yet." He rolled to his back and ran his hand over his thick cock, showing her just how weak he wasn't. "I see. What if I told you that you have guests downstairs and that I only came up here to check on you and to dress."

"Tell them to fuck off and then come back here and ride me." He wasn't wearing any pants either, he realized, and pulled the sheet off his naked body. "Ride me and forget the people downstairs."

He knew she was tempted, and when she licked her lips, he fisted his cock and held himself up for her to see. She took a step toward him, and he moaned. Christ, when she touched him he was going to come, he just knew it.

Crawling up his legs had his cock leaking. She didn't pause in her move up his body when she licked his crown clean. Reid wrapped his hand in her hair and held her there long enough for her to suckle him for a few minutes.

"We don't have time for this." He nodded. "It'll have to be quick. You can't dally because as soon as I have you inside me, I'm coming."

"Me too." When she straddled him, he grabbed her hips and guided her onto him. She was slow, agonizingly so. When he was buried to the root inside her, she started to ride him hard and fast. He leaned up and pulled her shirt off. Taking her nipple into his mouth, she curled her fingers in his hair.

"Come, Reid. Please. I need to feel you fill me." He rolled her to her back and pounded deep. "I'm coming."

She screamed out his name over and over as he came. His body needed more from her, and when he nuzzled her throat, she gave it to him. Before he could think about what he was doing, fangs dropped in his mouth and he bit into her vein.

Hot spicy blood filled his mouth. The faster he swallowed, the more he wanted. When she cried out again, coming tight around him, he lifted his head and looked down at her as he poured into her again.

Dropping down on her, he rolled to his back, taking her with him. It had been quick, but no less satisfying. When she shifted over him, sitting up over his cock, he held her hips still as she moved slowly. If she kept this up, he was going to come again.

"We really do need to go downstairs." She moaned when he pulled her tighter over him. "There are all kinds of people that want to talk to us together."

"They'll wait or not. I could care less." He sat up and suckled at her breast again before taking her mouth for a long drugging kiss. "You come with me again and I'll think about going down with you."

She pushed back to the bed and put her hands on his chest. Her breasts swayed to her movements as she rode him, and when she leaned back, filling her hands with her full breasts, he sat up again. As soon as she leaned into his shoulder, he moved his head, giving her what she'd given him earlier, and cried out when her teeth sank into his neck. Reid ran his fingers down her ass and found her tiny hole and slammed his finger deep. Her climax nearly took his breath away, and when he came too, stars burst behind his eyes. They both fell back on the bed and didn't move.

His heart was beginning to slow when he felt someone touching his mind. He was glad now that they'd not tried earlier because he was sure they'd have gotten an earful. It was Phil, and the man seemed to know what was delaying them.

"There are nineteen people here in your living room. Nancy has enlisted the help of a local girl to help make snacks, and you, my good man, are pissing them off by having a romp in the bed with your mate."

"Fuck off," he told the vampire. Phil laughed and asked him if they should expect them anytime soon. *"We're getting up now. I needed her, and as much as I'd like to tell you it's none of your business, I really needed her."*

"I understand. We'll be waiting."

CHAPTER 17

She was glowing. Austin wanted to talk to them both before everyone else did, and stood up as soon as they entered. But Jodie glowing startled him. CJ nudged him from behind, and he took a step toward them. Reid blocked him.

"Christ, you are too." Reid took a step back when Austin reached for him. He tried his best not to let it bother him, but pulled the man—because he was no longer a boy—into his arms. "I'm so sorry. More sorry than I've ever been for anything in my entire life. And trust me when I tell you I have a lot."

"You hurt her." Austin nodded, unable to talk around the large lump in his throat when Reid spoke. "She was going to leave me and it would have been your fault."

"I know, and I promise to make it up to her. Forever if that's what it takes." Austin let him go to look at Jodie. "I'm sorry for hurting you. I'm sorry for treating you like you were nothing to any of us. And I'm sorry for being an ass for the better part of the time we've known each other."

"You've been more than an ass and you know it." Her words hurt, but she smiled at him. "I guess I can forgive you. But the next time I won't be so—"

He jerked her to him and hugged her. The growl from Reid didn't bother him so much, but the one from CJ had him letting her go. She could be a little on the possessive side when she wanted to be. Austin put his arm around CJ and nodded. He had his family back now, and everything else in the world could fuck him. Austin Force was a happy man.

The man clearing his throat had him turning. He positioned himself in front of Reid and Jodie and pushed his wife behind him. He didn't know why he'd been summoned here, and he didn't know these yahoos, but they were not going to harm what was his.

"I'm alpha here, and this is my mate. I have no idea what you want with this couple, but I'll have you know that to get to them you'll have to go through me." He glanced at his brother Dallas when he stood up.

"And me." The rest of them stood as well, pushing Reid and Jodie to the back. Each of them, including mates, said that in order to get to the couple they were going to have to go through them as well. Phil walked up to stand in front of Austin and nodded to his mother.

"This is all well and good, but I believe that my mother has something to say as well. As does my father." Phil asked them all to have a seat and nodded toward the chairs when Jodie kept her stance. She was a fierce looking woman, and he decided that he wouldn't fuck with her if he were these guys.

"I'll stand, thanks." Jodie put her hands on her hips and glared at the three men that were beginning to rise. "That's far enough, thanks. Say what you have to say, then get the hell out of our house. We were having a nice little reunion when you showed up, and I'd like to get back to it."

"We've come to…." The oldest man cleared his throat twice before he looked at the woman standing next to him. When she nodded, he began again, only to be cut off when Jodie spoke, pointing to the only woman in the group.

"She's in charge. Let her do the talking." The woman smiled, and Austin had a feeling that it was a surprise to her to find humor in this. When she ask Jodie again to have a seat, she simply stood where she was.

"All right then. We've come to thank you for your years of service to us. Some of the things that you did for us had been a failure for so many before you. And when you took out the mage, you did us an even greater service."

"Get to the point." Austin had to cover his mouth when laughter threatened to erupt. The woman seemed taken aback by Jodie's bold statement. "As I've pointed out, I have things to do."

"So you did. As you are aware, you and your mate took out the mage. And in doing so received his great power. Didn't you?" Jodie didn't blink, and nothing about her body said a word either. "I see. You're not going to tell me anything are you? We've still come to offer you a job."

"No." Jodie sat down then, settling onto Reid's lap and holding him. Austin looked at the three people still standing there and wondered what they'd do to them if she didn't go and work for them.

"Perhaps I didn't make myself clear. You'd be working for us, and we'd pay you—"

"No, you explained yourself just fine. And the answer

195

is still the same. No. I don't want to work for you." The woman asked her why. "You are the ones that let this thing with the mage go on and on, knowing that he was killing other species. You didn't do shit when he hurt my father, and less than nothing when he killed my mother. I had to live with a sadist son of a bitch for nearly all my life because you didn't get up off your collective asses and do the right thing and bring him to heel. And don't even bother telling me that you didn't know. I can read your mind as well as you can anyone's."

"I can't read yours." The woman looked around. "I can't read anyone's mind in this room. Are you doing that?"

Austin looked at Jodie and wondered if she was. She, of course, said nothing to the woman and he doubted that she would. When the younger man stood up, he walked toward Jodie, and Austin stood up. He wasn't sure what was going to happen, but he wasn't going to hurt her.

"Take my hand, Jodie." She refused the man, and he looked at him. "Alpha, I'd very much like to give the young mage something if you'd allow it."

"In the event you didn't notice, she pretty much does what she wants. As for giving her something? I don't know that I would trust you either. She's right in saying you've done nothing to help her, and now you want her to work for you." Austin stood up and let a little of his wolf go. "I think it's time you guys left."

Hope stood up then and walked toward the three guests. "You've fucked this up royally, haven't you? Christ, why can't you guys just do what you're supposed to and leave all the mumbo jumbo out of it? Jodie, Reid, please come here."

Austin went as well. If things got nasty, then he was going to help them. There was no way he was going to sit by and let his pack be harmed by these people. When Hope turned and winked at him, he had a feeling she knew why he was there, and he felt better for it. She didn't send him away.

"This is Lady Marcum. She's the head honcho in charge of magic in this realm. She and I and a few others came here together long ago, and I'll tell you right now, she was a great deal less of a tight ass back then." The woman huffed at Hope as she continued. "This is Lord Peterson. He, too, came with us to this world, and he was less pompous then, but he's generally a good man. Peterson is in charge of managing the magic that vampires use. Though I bet it's been years since he's been out of his office to see to it. And this is Lord Titus. Titus is the son of a very wonderful couple who have since gone back to our world. Titus is the only one I trust."

"Now see here. You can't talk to us that way." Marcum sat back down hard after standing and screaming at them. Everyone turned to Jodie.

"She was being a pain in the ass again." When Jodie shrugged Marcum screamed at her to be let go and Jodie snapped her fingers. The woman disappeared. "I do want this over with, and she was not going to hurry along. Do I have to make myself clearer? I want to be alone with my mate."

"The job would be working for me," Titus said with a great deal of humor. "I'm in charge of all magic as it pertains to all species. This would include vampires now that Peterson has decided to retire. His replacement will be trained by me."

"Not me." Titus nodded when Jodie spoke. "Oh hell no. I'm not good with people and I hate them generally. Besides, in the event you didn't notice, I have a new mate."

"You do. And as such, he will be employed as well. When he can. I understand that you're a doctor." Reid nodded and looked at Austin.

"When I get my test scores back, I plan to work as doctor for the pack." The man reached into his coat pocket and handed him an envelope. Austin handed it to Reid when he saw who it was from. When Reid opened it, he sat down. "I passed. I really passed."

"You scored a perfect score is what you did." Titus looked at him. "Alpha, with your permission I'd like to have young Reid work for you, but in his off time, it would benefit us greatly if he could advise on a few cases when needed."

"You'll have to discuss that with them. As much as I'd like for him to do this for you, I'm not going to run his life. This is between the two of them." Austin looked at Reid as he continued talking to Titus. "But I will tell you this, you'll never have a finer man than this one, and if you can convince Jodie to work for you, you'll never have to worry about her loyalties, nor her ability to carry out her job."

"Thank you. I'm well aware of their abilities and what they received from the mage. Even before that, I was willing to have them come and work and train with us." He put out his hand to him, and Austin took it. "It's a great leader that gives someone what you just did."

Austin felt the magic surge over him. It nearly took his breath away when he staggered back. When CJ touched him, he felt his run from him to her, and Austin looked at Titus. The man smiled and turned to Reid and Jodie.

"In a few days I will return. Alone. We'll talk about your

198

options and how much I'd like for you to work for me." He bowed low and stood up. "Is Marcum somewhere safe or do I want to know?"

Jodie grinned and didn't answer. Austin was afraid to know where she'd sent the woman and decided that he'd never piss her off again. She was one scary woman.

~~~

Reid picked up the last glass and set it on the tray. The guests, or whatever they'd been, had left over an hour ago, and Jodie had started to clean up almost immediately. He didn't know what was wrong, but he could tell she was upset about something. When he entered the kitchen with the full tray, she was loading the dishwasher.

"I think we need to hire a cook. Someone to clean up, too, I think. This house is a little too big for the two of us to keep up with." He'd already hired a yard crew. After mowing for nearly five hours the first day, he'd not been able to make a dent in the yard. "Then I think we should consider having the pool worked on."

"I'm pregnant." She didn't stop loading the dishwasher as she continued. "I figured it out a little while ago when I was holding everyone's mind safe. Hope did it. Not the pregnant part but the fixing me part. She did it without telling me."

Reid sat down, trying not to touch her. He'd learned that when she was thinking she did it better without him touching her. She was thinking really hard right now.

"She told me when Ethan took you. The day that I'd told you that I could tell you were in heat is probably the day you conceived." She nodded but didn't comment. "I meant to tell you later, but it slipped my mind when you were riding me

199

like a stallion."

That had her pause putting a glass on the top rack of the machine. "Stallion, huh? Maybe more like a nice horse, but stallion?"

He reached for her when she slammed the door shut, pulling her onto his lap. "Perhaps you need another ride to make sure. Maybe you didn't get the full effect."

"You were in a hurry." She turned around and straddled his lap. She rode him now, their clothes making a delicious friction on his cock. When he cupped her ass and brought her closer, she moaned. "Are you going to hurry this time too?"

"Maybe this time, but once I get you to the bed, I plan to take my time." He sat her on the table and told her to lay back. Scooting his chair around, he pulled her pants off and touched the wet spot on her panties. "I'm hungry for you."

"Please." He tore her panties off and buried his nose in her pussy. When she moaned again, he took a small nip that had her rising up off the table.

"I'm going to eat my fill of you first. Then I'm going to fuck you right here." She moaned as he bit into her thigh. "After that I'm going to take you to our bedroom, tie you to the posts, and have my way with you again and again before I slam my cock into you and spill my seed."

Reid opened her nether lips and watched as her cream slid from her. Licking her from gate to clit, he suckled on her clit until her fingers curled into his hair. He bit her thigh again.

"Don't distract me from my work." She took her hands out of his hair and curled them around the edge of the table. When he seemed satisfied that she'd not touch him again, he went to work gorging himself on her. And she was a feast to be had.

Every time she came, he'd think this was the last time. He needed to fuck her, be buried deep inside of her. But she'd moan again, shifting on the table so that he'd need to taste another part of her. When she put her feet up on his shoulder, Reid nearly came in his pants, the view of her this way nearly perfect.

He had to free his cock, though, or hurt himself. Using his free hand, he opened his pants and pulled his cock out. He knew that he was close when his hand was covered in his own juices. Standing up, he pulled his jeans down and leaned over her. She ate his mouth when he kissed her as he'd done her pussy.

Reid moved his cock over her clit several times before he slammed deep. She arched up off the table, screaming. When she wrapped her legs around him, he rode her hard, pounding into her as hard as he could, sliding the table across the room.

"Come." He moaned when she shifted again. "Christ, Jodie, come for me. I need to fill you now."

She cried out and dug her nails into his back. Reid felt his own climax race up from his balls and spew from the tips as she sank her fangs into his shoulder. Crying out, he bit her shoulder as well, even as he felt a second climax take him by surprise. Drained and sated for now, he sealed the wound closed and dropped on her. Her giggle made him lift his head to look at her.

"You are getting really good at this biting thing. I thought you'd be a little squeemish." He'd never thought of it and told her that. "Yeah, I got that. I'm glad. I do need to feed once in a while, but when you bite me, it makes me come harder."

Reid picked her up in his arms and sat down in the chair again. He knew that he was going to stick to it and made a mental note to get cushions. She sighed and laid her head on his shoulder.

"What do you think about having a baby?" he asked her after several minutes. "I'm thrilled if you want to know the truth."

"Me too. But I worry. What if he's like me?" He lifted her chin and looked at her, trying to understand why that would be a problem. "I'm a shifter and we're not really accepted well."

"Bullshit. You're perfect, and if our daughter is anything like her mother, it's doubtful anyone will give her any shit about it." He sat her on the table and stood up. "Now, my dear mate, I'm going to lock up the house and make a payment on my promise to tie you to the bed."

She went up the stairs as he locked the front door. When someone knocked he was glad now that he'd pulled on his jeans. The man standing on the other side of the door didn't look like anyone he knew. Pulling the door open quickly had the human step back.

"I have a delivery for Mr. or Mrs. Reid Atkins. Would that be you?" Reid nodded and took the envelope. "Can you sign here?"

After signing his name, he reached for his wallet to tip the man when he realized it was in the kitchen with his shoes. The guy shook his head, telling him that he'd been taken care of and left. When the car was out of sight, Reid shut the door and set the alarm. He was nearly to the bedroom when he looked at the envelope.

"Do you know any one by the name of 'T. Shipwreck'?" She told him no from the closed bathroom door. "We just got something from them."

She came out of the bathroom wearing a towel and nothing else. He crumpled the envelope in his hand when she walked toward him. She took the envelope and danced away while he stood there trying to get his brain to work again. When she stopped suddenly and turned to him, he was almost afraid to ask.

"It's from Titus. He said that we were to receive the reward for taking care of Ethan. He sent us a check." She held it out to him, and he put his hands behind his back. Her face, shocked and a little afraid, told him he didn't want to know. "You have to see it. It's made out to us both."

"Tell me." She shook her head. "Please tell me. Is it a lot? A little? Are there a lot of zeros?"

Her answer of a simple yes was no help at all. When she shoved it into his hand, he had no choice but to look then, and he had to sit down. The accompanying letter didn't help either. Jodie started to read it to him when he kept staring at the check.

"Reid and Jolene, I hope that this letter finds you well and full of questions. The check enclosed is only for your help in dealing with the mage. I should have given it to you while we were there. But, alas, I forgot in all the excitement.

"I would like to tell you that this money is for services rendered. The money that you'll be making for us will be a great deal more."

Reid put up his hand to stop Jodie from reading any more. "What does he mean 'a great deal more'? More than this?" She said apparently so. Reid pulled her to him and kissed her. "Enough, woman. I want you on the bed now."

CHAPTER 18

"Do you think they'll do it?" CJ looked at her mate in the mirror. He was so handsome he took her breath away. "Hope said that it paid well."

"I don't know. She seemed pretty set on not doing it. Titus did ask me if there was fee they had to give me when they were paid. You think he's going to pay them for killing Ethan?"

She shrugged. CJ knew that the house that Reid had bought was paid for. She'd helped Tristan go to the bank and do it. The man had also put their names on the deeds to several of his houses, as well as on a substantial bank account. She told Austin.

"Then that takes a great burden off him. I know he has some pretty stiff student loans to pay back. And when I suggested that the pack pay them, he said that he'd rather they didn't. He's a good man."

CJ turned to look at him. She wondered if he knew what a great man he was as well, and decided that he more than likely didn't. She stood up and sat on the edge of the bed while he got undressed.

"Do you know what they'll have to do working for

Titus?" Austin said he didn't. "I asked Hope. She told me that Jodie would be like their enforcer and that Reid would be asked to sometimes help her out when the case was big. They will be asked to fight people like Ethan was."

"Honestly? I hope they don't take it. With Jodie having a baby, I think it would be great if they could just be couple. I don't even think they have any help in that house of theirs either."

Reid had asked her and Nancy to help him out with that too. He said he didn't want his mate worn out all the time trying to keep it up. He'd even hired a newly formed lawn service that she and Austin used. The man was getting his head together.

"I don't think I want them to either. I think like you that being a parent will be enough for them. Especially since they never thought they'd have any kids." When Austin was ready for bed, she got up to go to the other side. As soon as they were under the blankets, she rolled to him and settled herself over his body. He held her as he did every night. "Austin, what if I told you I'd like to have another baby?"

"I'd say you were insane and that we just got the last one in school." He didn't move for several seconds. "Do you think we could have another little girl? I just love little girls in the house. Of course, a son wouldn't be so bad either. How about one of each?"

CJ sat up on his chest and stared at him. "I don't know what we're having yet. I've only just found out today that I was."

He nodded and held her. CJ waited for his mind to catch up to what she'd said. When it did, she nearly wet herself laughing at him.

"You're pregnant now?" She nodded. "I don't understand. You just asked me if I wanted to have a baby. And you're already pregnant?"

He got up to pace the room, and she laughed. "Actually I was pregnant before I asked you, so I didn't suddenly get this way. And if memory serves me right, and you know that it always does, you were a big part of me being in this condition anyway."

Austin stopped pacing to stare at her. "You're really going to have another baby? Our baby?"

"Yes. Are you happy with this?" He shook his head, and she felt her heart crush. "I'm having this baby. I'm not going to—"

He put his hand over her mouth as he crawled back into the bed with her. "I'm not just happy, I'm ecstatic. I've never been happier in my life."

When CJ lay back down with him, she had to fight the tears. She'd been so worried that he'd be upset. Their other children were in school now so having a baby meant they would have to start all over. She smiled when she thought of the look on Nancy's face when she found out.

"I love you, CJ. I've never in all my life loved anyone as much as I do you." She did cry now, the tears flowing from her eyes like a fountain. He lifted her chin up to look at her. "I'm sorry, honey. I didn't mean to upset you."

"I'm just so happy right now." He held her while she cried. "Austin, never change. Please. Just stay the same loveable man you are right now. Okay?"

"Okay, love, but I got to tell you, it's hard being this

perfect all the time." She slapped him and closed her eyes. It had been a long week, and she was exhausted.

~~~

Tristan knew that he'd have to see her sooner or later, but right now he had his hands full. When his new cell phone rang, he nearly ignored it, but picked it up just before it went to voice mail.

"Well?" He would have to figure out how to make sure that he knew who was calling him from now on. Tristan didn't want to have to talk to Hope just yet.

"Well what?" She laughed. "You should know that I've been meaning to come and see you. I've been busy setting up my house."

It had been set up the day after he'd moved in. His magic had seen to that, and he was reasonably sure that Hope knew it. When he started to tell her that he had to go, she spoke again.

"Good, since you have a nice house, we'll be right over." The phone went dead, and before he could think to leave his house, she was knocking on the door. Tristan stomped to the door and swung it open.

"I'm not ready to talk to you yet." She, of course, ignored him and went into the main hall, looking around as she went. Her husband, Rod, walked by him and winked. He was not in the mood for either of them.

"You should know that I've spoken to your daughter. And she is as pigheaded as you are." For some reason, Tristan thought of it as a compliment, not the insult he was sure she'd meant for it to be. "And she and Reid shouldn't take that job. That's why we're here."

"What?" He followed them, now anxious to see why they agreed with him. "You don't want her to take the job. Why the bloody hell not?"

He flushed when she raised a brow at him, but she answered him. "Because she's done enough for our kind and needs to simply be a woman. And I would have thought you'd agree with me."

"I do." She sat down, and he sat across from her. Rod stood near the fire place. "As much as I hate to admit to agreeing with you, I do on this. She and Reid can have a good life and one that doesn't involve all this…." He waved his hand in the air, hoping she'd understand what he meant. Apparently she did.

"They are a lovely couple, and the fact that she's so powerful makes me know that they'll have a long and happy life together." He didn't like the way she said that and asked her what she meant. "I know what you did to them. When they were both healing from this last ordeal. You gave them life."

Tristan flushed. He'd done more than that, but he didn't answer her. Instead, he turned the tables on them. Rod burst out laughing, and Hope flushed. "What about what you did to them? At least mine was given to my daughter. You barged right in there and took away a gift I should have given them."

"I didn't know you cared." They were standing toe to toe when Rod cleared his throat. They both turned to him and glared. Rod simply asked them to sit on the couch.

"You do know that whatever you've given them is going to be secondary to what they already have, don't you?" They both nodded. "And so you know, I had a talk with Titus before he left the house today. They've both been paid for the job they did for the magic world. Quite well as a matter of fact."

"How well?" Tristan wasn't happy when Rod only smiled. "You gave them some money too. Did you happen to think I might like to contribute some to the pot?"

These two were going to drive him nuts. And he had a feeling he wasn't going to be the only grandparent to the baby either. Damn it, they were going to horde in on his time with the little baby. When Rod handed him a sheet of paper, he smiled. This he could help them with.

As soon as they left, he set to work on the list. First off was the new clinic for the pack. If he was going to live here from now on, they'd need the best. Especially if his grandchild was going to be born in it. By the time the sun was nearly half way across the sky he'd done it all and had spent a great deal of money. More than they'd been given in that check. Fifty million was a lot of money, but what he'd done was going to be fantastic.

As he laid to rest, he smiled. This was going to be a great deal of fun trying to outdo the Campbell's. But he had something that they'd never have and that was blood. His daughter was going to make him a grandfather. He was closing his eyes when something occurred to him. Getting up, he picked up the phone and called Reid.

"Are you going to marry her soon?" Reid didn't answer him fast enough, and he launched into all the reasons why he'd better get on the stick. "She will not have your bastard. You want her to stay there with you, then I would suggest that you make her your wife before you have sex with her."

"Sir, I don't know if you realize this or not, but in order for her to have gotten pregnant, we've had sex." Tristan growled at Reid. "But we are planning a nice, quiet wedding this weekend. Just the family. I think Jodie was going to call you today to let you know."

That appeased him. For now. "You'll not be doing anything with my little girl until you're married. Do you understand me?" Reid assured him that he did, but didn't commit to anything. Then he called Jolene and told her the same things. It was time that he put his foot down as a father. He was just closing his eyes when his daughter appeared in his room.

"You overbearing, pompous asshole. Where do you get off telling me when I can have sex? And calling my mate in the middle of the day when he's trying to work and bothering him with this makes me want to punch you in the nose." She looked at him, then around the room. He had no idea what she was looking for until she slapped her hand over her mouth and ran to his bathroom. He was standing near the door when Reid finally showed up.

"She just started throwing up. I was going to call an ambulance, but she threatened me. Threatened me with all sorts of bodily harm." Reid knocked on the door, and he was ready to tell him that she wasn't letting anyone in when the door opened. He tried to slip in when she snarled at him.

Twenty minutes later, they came out and he was aghast at how pale Jolene was. He had her sit down and held her hand. She jerked from him and glared again.

"I don't think you should be doing that. The baby needs quiet and peacefulness." She snarled at him something he'd

211

never heard before, and he backed up, looking at Reid. "I think she's possessed. Maybe that baby is taking over her body?"

"She's only having a bit of morning sickness." Tristan pointed out that it was nearly four o'clock. "Well, when she's stressed, she gets sick too. I didn't think it would start this early in the pregnancy, but all babies are different. Jodie needs for you not to stress her out."

"Me?" When she tried to launch herself at him, Tristin still had his doubt that she wasn't possessed. She looked wild. "I will refrain from making demands on you."

When she stood up, he wasn't sure she was going to kill him or not and decided his best course of action was to remain still, like a wounded animal. Jodie glared at him again before she took a step over him and moved out of the room. He looked at Reid.

"She'll be fine. I'm going to have to go back to work now, but from now on perhaps you should call me instead of letting her know what you've said. She's a might touchy about this wedding thing."

After they left, he decided to get a couple of books on women having babies. He'd feel better if he was more equipped at handling things. Tristan thought he might suggest he move in with them for a little while. He was sure that Reid could take care of her when he was there, but the poor thing looked like she might have killed him. Her own father. Tristan moved out into the darkening yard and thought about what a gift he'd been given.

"Ah, Kelley my love, you should see her. Spitting image of you when we met. And that Reid? He's a man that I would

212

have picked for her if I'd had the chance." He didn't lie to his wife, in life or death. "I think I might have upset her a little today. I'll try my best to keep my options to myself." He smiled when a sharp breeze blew over him. "Okay, you know I did say try."

For several minutes, he watched the lowering sun before he spoke to her again. "I know I said I wanted to come to you, but I'd like to spend some time with this new family they're creating. I love you dearly, and I promise you that I'll have such grand stories to tell you when I come to you. And the child will want for nothing."

Tristan pulled out his list and looked it over. "I've bought them a few things. And given them a few more. The house that you loved, I've given them, and the money. What use have I for it, I ask you? I've been around longer than most stones and haven't used any of what we had. After buying this house and a few things, I've still fifty times more than we started with long ago." He slipped the list into his pocket, ever so grateful that Rod had given it to him.

"Hope and Rod Campbell are here as well. You remember them, don't you? She's still as bossy as ever, and he's just as calm. I suppose he'd have to be to put up with her all these years." Another breeze blew over him. This one cool. "I know you put up with a great deal from me too. I didn't mean I wasn't happy they were here. Just letting you know."

He was happy they were here. Hope had always been one to have fun teasing and pissing off, and Rod was a great man simply to talk about books with. He told Kelley about the book and giving it to Hope.

213

"I'll think about the other book. I've had it so long now that…well, I'm not ready to give it up yet. Maybe that other boy, Randy, can help me with it. He's a lawyer, you know. Or he's going to be. Maybe he can be the one to help lay out the laws in it before I give it to him." He looked at the swaying trees. "He's a good boy. Sharp too. The few times I've talked to him, he's impressed me as a man who wants to go far. Mayhap I can horde in on a couple more grandchildren for us to look down on."

He'd have to spend more time with Randy, he decided. Get to know the boy before things in the book started to show themselves. He supposed he could have gone to Phil with them, but what fun would that be? New blood was what they needed now.

"Yes, my dear, I think I'll hang around here for a little while longer. Just to see how all this turns out. You never know, maybe I can convince someone to name a baby after me and you."

ABOUT THE AUTHOR

Kathi Barton, author of the bestselling series Force of Nature, lives in Nashport, Ohio with her husband Paul. In addition to writing full time Kathi likes to spend time with her eight grandkids, three children and three children-in-laws. She writes to relax and have fun. Her muse, a cross between Jimmy Stewart and Hugh Jackman brings them to life for her readers in a way that has them coming back time and again for more. Her favorite genre is paranormal romance with a great deal of spice. You can visit Kathi on line and drop her an email if you'd like. She loves hearing from her fans. aaronskiss@gmail.com. Follow Kathi on her blog:
http://kathisbartonauthor.blogspot.com/